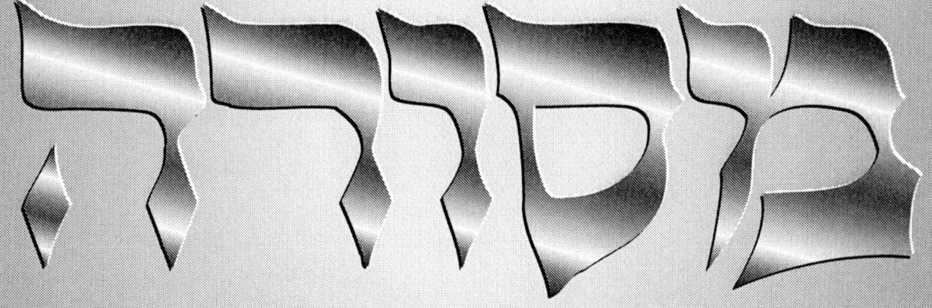

ArtScroll® Youth Series

Rabbi Nosson Scherman / Rabbi Meir Zlotowitz

General Editors

A MYSTERY FROM AFAR

Published by
Mesorah Publications, ltd

AND OTHER

LEAH LAMDAN HOLIDAY MYSTERIES

by

CHAYA HUBNER

FIRST EDITION
Two Impressions ... November 2007 — August 2013
Third Impression ... August 2018

Published and Distributed by
MESORAH PUBLICATIONS, LTD.
4401 Second Avenue / Brooklyn, N.Y 11232

Distributed in Europe by
LEHMANNS
Unit E, Viking Business Park
Rolling Mill Road
Jarow, Tyne & Wear, NE32 3DP
England

Distributed in Australia and New Zealand by
GOLDS WORLDS OF JUDAICA
3-13 William Street
Balaclava, Melbourne 3183
Victoria, Australia

Distributed in Israel by
SIFRIATI / A. GITLER — BOOKS
POB 2351
Bnei Brak 51122

Distributed in South Africa by
KOLLEL BOOKSHOP
Northfield Centre, 17 Northfield Avenue
Glenhazel 2192, Johannesburg, South Africa

ARTSCROLL® YOUTH SERIES
A MYSTERY FROM AFAR AND OTHER LEAH LAMDAN HOLIDAY MYSTERIES

ISBN 10: 1-4226-0611-2 / ISBN 13: 978-1-4226-0611-7 (hard cover)
ISBN 10: 1-4226-0612-0 / ISBN 13: 978-1-4226-0612-4 (paperback)

Typography by CompuScribe at ArtScroll Studios, Ltd.

Printed in the United States of America
Bound by Sefercraft, Quality Bookbinders, Ltd., Brooklyn N.Y. 11232

TABLE OF CONTENTS

JUDGMENT DAY

AN EREV ROSH HASHANAH MYSTERY

It was just before 8 o'clock on a Monday morning toward the end of September. Because it was Erev Rosh Hashanah, there was no school that day, so Leah Lamdan was quietly eating her breakfast when her father returned from davening Shacharis.

"Up already?" he asked as he placed the bag containing his tallis and tefillin on a stand outside the dining room and walked into the kitchen. He found his coffee mug and began to fill it with steaming hot water.

"It's a matter of getting used to," she said. Her reply was crisp and definite. "I always get up at 7 o'clock, shower, dress, daven, and eat breakfast. Then I just have to figure out what I'll be doing for the rest of the day." A bright flush stained her cheeks. "But today I know — I have to get ready for Rosh Hashanah."

Rabbi Lamdan frowned. He turned away from her as he added a little instant coffee to his mug, and then joined her at the table. He almost managed a wry smile. "*I'm* going to court, this morning. Would you like to join me?"

Leah looked surprised. Her blue eyes widened. She remained focused on his face as she leaned toward him and said, "Isn't it ironic that today, on Erev Rosh Hashanah, the day before Judgment Day in the Heavenly Court, you are going to a secular court? What happened?"

He chuckled at her response and shook his head in amusement. His face, however, looked grim. "Reb Aharon Cohen was arrested last week for carrying a concealed weapon. The law clearly states that it is illegal to carry a loaded gun except in one's home or place of business unless one has a special 'carry permit.' The law does state, however, that you are permitted to carry an unloaded gun, such as a rifle, as long as it has to be assembled before being used. Since Reb Aharon had a loaded gun in his station wagon, he needs character witnesses to vouch that he is an honest and good man."

"Today of all days, Erev Rosh Hashanah, he has to go to court!" she said sardonically. "And why, if I may ask, did he have a gun in his car?"

"Reb Aharon says that it's not his gun. He doesn't know how it got into the armrest of his car. He bought the car secondhand about four months ago from Avraham Cohen, who moved with his family to Israel. This Avraham Cohen was a jewelry salesman, and probably had a permit to carry a gun to protect himself from robbers. Reb Aharon doesn't need a gun, though. He travels around selling sefarim from the car. You can always find him parked in front of shuls and yeshivahs, selling all kinds of sefarim."

He drew his brows into a tight frown as he studied Leah intently.

His cell phone rang and he answered, speaking quickly into the phone as he glanced toward Leah. "Want to see an American court in action?" he asked her.

"Sure," she replied. "This is a most interesting thing to do on Erev Rosh Hashanah! But how did Reb Aharon get into this mess in the first place?"

"Reb Aharon is a talmid chacham and an eidel, refined person. He was driving along when a policeman stopped him and told him that he had a broken taillight on his station wagon. Since he had stopped the car already, the officer decided to check Reb Aharon's license and registration. Reb Aharon looked in the glove compartment but could not find the registration, so he looked in the armrest. As he was removing the junk that had been left inside, he saw the gun — which he says he never saw before — and took that out, too. When the policeman saw the gun, he immediately took it away from Reb Aharon and it was inevitable that he was arrested for possession."

"But he wasn't using it!" Leah stared soberly at her father.

"Baruch Hashem for that! Why should he, chas v'shalom, have to use a gun? He is only charged with carrying it. That's the stringency of the law. He had no right to have it with him, even if he wasn't using it."

"But you said that he said that he didn't even know that he had it." Her face brightened because she was confident that Reb Aharon would be freed immediately.

"Yes, I did," he replied. He nodded, his eyes never leaving her face. "I did say that, but the police don't believe him, because they checked their records and found that the gun is owned by A. Cohen."

"Avraham Cohen, the previous owner," Leah deduced. It was obvious to her what had happened.

"We're trying to find Avraham Cohen in Israel but it's like looking for a needle in a haystack," her father sighed. "In any event, today is the court hearing and this is no simple matter."

Mrs. Lamdan came into the kitchen and smiled faintly at her husband and daughter. "You look serious this morning." She clasped her hands and stared from one to the other. She turned to Rabbi Lamdan and raised an eyebrow. "Have you heard any more about Reb Aharon? Did they find Avraham Cohen?"

Rabbi Lamdan shook his head, hope struggling with fear in his expression. "Nothing new," he said. "We just have to daven that everything will be all right." A grin transformed his face. "Perhaps now everything *will* go smoothly."

◇◇◇

When they reached the courthouse, they saw an older man standing near the door, attempting to blow a shofar. He clearly did not know that one does not blow the shofar outside and that, although the shofar is blown daily during the month of Elul to remind people to do teshuvah, it is not sounded on Erev Rosh Hashanah. The officers outside the courthouse ignored the man because he was unsuccessful; his shofar was silent. "Rosh Hashanah is here," he announced between puffs. "It is Judgment Day. Ask forgiveness from Hashem."

Rabbi Lamdan and Leah spotted Moshe Moskowitz, the lawyer, with his shoulders hunched and his hands jammed into his pockets, talking to some other men whom Leah recognized as important members of their community.

"Are they also character witnesses?" whispered Leah. It was then that she noticed Mrs. Cohen, Reb Aharon's wife, who had pulled a wad of tissues from her purse and was wiping her eyes.

"You've got to understand," Leah heard her say to another woman who was standing beside her. "Aharon is innocent of any wrongdoing ...."

"Just tell him to give a little more tzedakah today," said the other woman. "I am donating in his name and I have asked others to do the same."

"What kind of trial will it be?" Leah asked, turning to her father. "Are they calling a jury?"

"There's no trial yet, Leah," he explained. "Today's procedure is a hearing to determine if a crime was committed. The facts will be presented to a judge instead of to a jury. That could be good for Reb Aharon, because a judge might be sympathetic, based on Reb Aharon's character and clean record, and dismiss the case. After all, it's pretty clear that no crime was committed." Rabbi Lamdan began to twist a few strands of his beard, a sign that he was nervous about his friend and about the outcome of this trial.

They entered the courtroom. "Reb Aharon's is not the first case on the docket," Rabbi Lamdan told his daughter. "We can observe the other cases until his turn is called. Then I will have to wait in the corridor until I am summoned into the courtroom by the court clerk." He indicated a stern-faced white-haired man in a gray suit.

When Judge Stein entered the courtroom, the clerk ordered everyone to stand respectfully until the judge took his seat and the hearings began. An hour dragged by. Leah listened carefully to each of the cases. She found it rather interesting, but her father was becoming anxious.

It would soon be noon and the judge would call a recess for lunch. Rabbi Lamdan wanted to be home by lunchtime because he needed time to prepare for Rosh Hashanah. He looked toward the others who had come to speak for Reb Aharon and saw the anxiety written on their faces, too. Just then, Moshe Moskowitz hurried into the courtroom, moving toward Leah's father and the other men. He signaled them to follow him out into the hall and they all stood up to leave. At first, Leah wasn't sure what to do, but then her father told her to stay in her seat and watch the proceedings carefully.

Reb Aharon was brought into the courtroom. He sat down at a table designated by Moshe Moskowitz. The prosecutor stood at another table with a folder in front of him, and called for the arresting officer to testify.

The officer related the facts, including the information that Reb Aharon seemed surprised to find the gun in the armrest. But, since Reb Aharon was not allowed to have a gun in his possession, he had to be arrested.

"Was the gun loaded?" the prosecutor asked.

The arresting officer nodded. "He was caught red-handed. He claimed that he knew nothing about the gun and that it wasn't his. I took him back to the station house and we checked it out. We discovered that the gun was registered in his name."

The prosecutor nodded in satisfaction and took his seat. Then it was Moshe Moskowitz's turn. He stood up to question the arresting officer and asked him the name of the registered owner of the gun. The officer flipped through his notepad and read aloud, "The gun was registered to A. Cohen."

Moshe Moskowitz looked at him and frowned. "How do you know that A. Cohen is Aharon Cohen? Maybe it's

Abraham Cohen or Albert Cohen? You are using circumstantial evidence to accuse my client!"

The officer did not look happy. He stared coldly at Mr. Moskowitz and replied, "I — I don't know why — I guess I forgot to write the full name in my notebook. Call it what you want — I know that Aharon Cohen had the gun."

Mr. Moskowitz folded his arms across his chest. He stood straight and slim, his kind face furrowed by a thoughtful frown. "Before you saw the gun, which Mr. Cohen gave you willingly, did he seem belligerent or argumentative?"

The officer looked unperturbed. "No. He was calm and told me that he sells Hebrew books. That he traveled from religious institution to religious institution with the kind of books that they need." While speaking, anger hardened his voice.

"So, you don't like religious institutions?" asked Reb Aharon's lawyer.

The officer shifted in his seat. His exasperation was clear. He tried to keep his tone pleasant. "That's not why I stopped him and that's not why I arrested him. People shouldn't travel around our great country with guns — loaded guns — in their possession. That's how people get hurt. People who break the law have to be put away. They belong in prison."

After the officer was excused and stepped down from the witness stand, Mr. Moskowitz called Leah's father and then each of the other friends to the witness stand to testify about Reb Aharon's fine character and complete honesty. Finally, he called Reb Aharon to the witness stand. He repeated essentially the same facts that the officer had related.

Suddenly they heard what sounded like an alarm of some kind. Everyone stood, looked around, and began moving out of the courtroom. Reb Aharon was taken out through a side door by a court officer and Judge Stein went into his chambers. While they were waiting in the corridor, Leah turned to her father and asked him a question.

Rabbi Lamdon listened to what she was saying and nodded. He walked over to Moshe Moskowitz and spoke to him. The lawyer looked back toward Leah and smiled. Meanwhile, the other officers had found the old man who had finally managed to blow his shofar outside one of the courtroom windows. The old man had not realized that he was disrupting the case and he promised not to blow the shofar again near the courthouse. As the officers led him away, he called out loudly, "Do teshuvah, people! You must do teshuvah!"

Everyone re-entered the courtroom. Judge Stein returned to his seat. The prosecuting attorney stood up to give his brief closing argument, during which he strongly stated his opinion that Reb Aharon should go to prison.

Then Mr. Moskowitz stood up to give his closing argument. "Your Honor, we seem to be faced with a terrible situation here today. The accused was found with a loaded gun in his possession, a gun that, according to law, he is not allowed to keep except in his home or his place of business."

"We know this already, Counselor," interrupted the judge. "Are you throwing the accused on the mercy of the court?"

Moshe Moskowitz turned his head and smiled at Leah. Then he turned back to the judge and shook his head. "Really, Your Honor, I wish to maintain that Aharon Cohen has the right to carry the gun because his station wagon *is* his place of business."

There was a hush in the courtroom. Judge Stein glared at Moshe Moskowitz and then began to smile. He looked thoughtful as he tented his fingers on his desk and stared ahead. "You maintain that since the station wagon is his place of business, he should be permitted to carry the gun?" It was a rhetorical question. The judge nodded and turned to Reb Aharon.

He struck the desk with his gavel. "Case dismissed," he announced. "Let's break for lunch now. Have a good year, everyone." Leah was sure that the judge winked at Mr. Moskowitz before leaving the courtroom.

Leah's father stood and rushed over to Reb Aharon to shake his hand. Reb Aharon looked as if he were in a daze. Moshe Moskowitz smiled and shook Rabbi Lamdan's hand. He smiled back at Leah. "Thank you, thank you," he repeated. "May you be zocheh to much nachas and many, many simchos!"

A Message From A Friend

An Aseres Yemei Teshuvah Mystery

Leah heard the phone ringing late in the evening while she was trying to relax after a long, difficult day. It was one of the *Aseres Yemei Teshuvah*, the Ten Days of Repentance between Rosh Hashanah and Yom Kippur. This was the time of year when she tried to find additional mitzvos to do. Sometimes she liked to express her thoughts verbally to hear if they sounded all right. But today her attention was transfixed, albeit begrudgingly, by something else.

"Why now?" she asked aloud. Today was one of those difficult days because she was grieving. A dear friend's grandfather, who was close to all the Lamdans, had suddenly passed away. Binyamin "Yummy" Gartner had just joined the ranks of the retired and was planning a trip to Israel with his wife, Temimah. He was also the "lollipop man" in shul and it was the youngsters in shul who had nicknamed him "Yummy." He often gave "Leah the Lamdan" a special lollipop to "sweeten the truth." He had always had a smile, a laugh, and a lollipop. Everyone had been thrilled that he had finally made arrangements to visit Israel. That was one reason that the suddenness of his passing was so profoundly sad.

Leah had not only gone to the levayah but had received special permission to attend the burial at the Bais Olom Cemetery as well. She could not postpone her grief, but these days before Yom Kippur didn't seem to be the right time to confront the reality of death.

To calm herself, Leah took several slow, deep breaths. She noticed the tantalizing aroma of an apple-spice cake her mother was baking. She emerged from her self-imposed exile in her room and made her way into the kitchen. "Hi, Ima, that smells delicious," she said. "I even smelled it up in my room."

Mrs. Lamdan sighed. She remained silent for a moment before saying, "I made two cakes, one for us and one for Yummy's family." She still couldn't change the way she had referred to him for so long.

There was a small silence. Leah broke it, her voice more serious. "I'll take it over to them," she murmured reassuringly. "You won't have to go over till later in the shivah." But she was filled with apprehension. She felt her hand tremble just a little as she cut a small piece from one of the cakes. She was still feeling stress from a very hectic week.

On Rosh Hashanah, Leah had been enchanted by the *piyyutim*, the liturgy of the machzor. In fact, her machzor was on the kitchen table, as she had been reviewing the beautiful liturgical poems. She was especially drawn to the hymns of Rabbi Eliezer ibn (ben) Kalir, also known as Eliezer HaKalir, who was one of the earliest and prolific *paytanim*, poets. His poems can be found in the Tishah B'Av Kinnos and in the machzorim of Rosh Hashanah and Yom Kippur. His works are enriched with words and expressions that convey our feelings toward Hashem. Leah was intrigued because little is known about him, although it is assumed that he lived in Kiryas Sefer in Israel sometime between the sixth and tenth centuries. Some say that he was the son of Rabbi Shimon Bar Yochai, one of the Sages of the Mishnah. Others say that he was the Rabbi Eliezer ben Shimon who is mentioned in the Medrash on Sefer Vayikra. The acrostics in his hymns usually refer to his father's name, Kalir. Rashi quotes Ibn Kalir's poems in his Tanach and Talmud commentaries. A street near the city council building in Tel Aviv is named for him.

Leah remembered asking her father about Eliezer ibn Kalir after a Tishah B'Av fast. Her father told her that the meaning of the name "Kalir" is not known, and that some say that his name was adopted as a surname, "HaKalir." Others say that "kalir" means cake and that Rabbi Eliezer had eaten a certain kind of cake that was a segulah for attaining wisdom.

As Leah was remembering her Rosh Hashanah musing, the doorbell rang. Leah glanced at her watch and went to the door. She was surprised to find the familiar figure of Police Lieutenant McCarthy on the doorstep, nervously switching his briefcase from hand to hand. Leah opened the door and greeted him.

"Hi, Lieutenant. Do you need help with another case?" she asked, smiling broadly.

The lieutenant smiled back and asked, "May I have a word with you? Is this a bad time to call?"

"Come in," Leah replied. "My mother is in the kitchen."

He followed her into the kitchen where Mrs. Lamdan was seated at the table, wrapping the cake to be sent to the Gartners' home. With a troubled look on her face, she said, "Lieutenant, whom do you wish to speak to? Is it me, my husband, or Leah?"

"Whoever can answer my question," he responded, forcing a smile although he seemed disappointed. Before knocking on their door, he had convinced himself that one of the Lamdans would be available to answer his questions and solve the problem that had stumped him and his staff. But just as he rang the doorbell, he said to himself, *Nonsense! This is ridiculous!* He had been about to turn away when Leah opened the door. Now, in the kitchen, he looked from mother to daughter and smiled bemusedly.

They waited patiently for him to begin, and Mrs. Lamdan offered him a piece of the spice cake, put out some coffee, and dropped a piece of lemon near the cup. Nodding, his expression serious, he sat down, placed his briefcase on his knees, and began to speak. "A close friend of mine works for the Federal government. He was kidnapped by terrorists who are threatening to kill him tomorrow if we don't free certain prisoners held by our government."

At that moment, Rabbi Lamdan walked into the kitchen to join them. Lieutenant McCarthy quickly told him about the kidnapping. Frowning, Rabbi Lamdan exclaimed. "What do you mean? Are these terrorists in New York?"

Lieutenant McCarthy, trying to swallow his coffee and speak at the same time, caught his breath and cleared his throat. "Give me a few minutes," he said, "and I will explain .... My friend, Loser Keller, was always a winner. You know, sometimes a nickname is based on opposites, like calling a tall kid, 'Shorty.' Well, on that basis, Loser was really a winner. I can't think of any other reason he was called *Loser*. There were many times when the enemy almost caught him, but he always managed to escape. This time, regrettably, they got him and they're threatening our government, stating that unless we give up many of our prisoners, they won't let Loser live."

Rabbi Lamdan paled. "You know," he said, "The State of Israel has promised its soldiers that they will always bring them back. No soldier has to worry that he will be kept by the enemy, dead or alive. Israel has made prisoner exchanges such as 'one of ours for 250 of theirs.' Other countries marvel that we do such things, but every soldier is a Yiddishe neshamah — a Jewish soul — and we can not allow our fellow Jew to languish among those who would do harm."

"So our government is ready to negotiate, too," the lieutenant continued, "but that won't stop us from trying to get him back before the negotiations are complete." Settling back, relaxing a little, his thoughts momentarily strayed. "I remember Loser very well. He was some smart guy! He was addicted to all kinds of puns and puzzles. That's why he was so good at his job. He makes and breaks codes for our government."

"So, what do you want from us?" asked Rabbi Lamdan. "You don't think that he is hidden here somewhere in our Jewish community, do you?"

"That's not the issue," McCarthy went on. "The American government knows plenty about these terrorists. We know even the hideouts they use to hold their captives. We're pretty good at that." At last a small smile formed on his lips.

"So what's the problem?" asked Leah. "Just go in and get him!" Her father and mother concurred with her line of reasoning and they expressed their agreement with pride and pleasure.

"If only it were so easy," Lieutenant McCarthy sighed. "But it's not. We don't know where he is, exactly. We only know that here in Brooklyn there is a possibility that Loser is being held in one of five places. We cannot allow the terrorists to know that we have a list of their hideouts, so we can't attack all five hideouts at the same time. Besides that, we have to use too many trained men for a series of raids like that. We can't insure Loser's safety by making five raids, because one of the terrorists may escape and warn the others before we get to the right hideout. Only when we know exactly where Loser is can we take the chance of launching a raid."

Everyone nodded in agreement. Leah looked at her father and held back a smile, endeavoring to keep a straight face. "So what do you want *us* to do?"

"I want to show you a video and I would like your impression of it."

Leah was startled by his request.

McCarthy continued. "The terrorists have sent us a video message from Loser. He is requesting that we help him and that we do whatever they want to secure his freedom." His facial muscles twitched nervously.

"You think they tortured him so that he would make this request against his will?" asked Mrs. Lamdan.

"Yes, but I also think that he is sending us a message to let us know where he is," Lieutenant McCarthy said as he stared at Leah. "He used a certain hand-signal that means he is being coerced into saying these words."

"Where are these five hideouts?" asked Leah. "We would have to know that in order to figure out any hidden message in what Loser says."

The lieutenant grunted in assent. He reached into his briefcase and pulled out a paper. "If you reveal what I am about to show you, I will lose my job," he said. "I trust all of you, but others don't know how much you have helped me in the past. They would question my actions, so please let us keep this information only in this room."

The Lamdans all nodded in agreement as he placed the sheet of paper on the table. "The first place is on East 13th Street in Flatbush. The second is on Franklin Avenue in Crown Heights. The third is on Division Avenue in Williamsburg. The fourth is on Louisa Street, bordering Kensington and Borough Park. And the last is on East 98th Street in Canarsie."

Leah frowned. "It means nothing to me," she said. She sounded tired.

Her father looked at her with a sad expression on his face. "I know how you feel. Nothing registers with me, either."

McCarthy took a video camera from his briefcase, set it on the table, and inserted a video disk. He flicked the switch and the video began to play on the camera's small screen. The projected picture was not clear at first. Many lines ran across the screen before the image finally settled and focused on a man's face. The man — about Rabbi Lamdan's age — looked unkempt and very tired. He moved his left hand in a pained motion. He spoke in a low voice and he looked bewildered by the situation he was in. He did not stare into the camera lens, but rather looked toward one of the kidnappers and said hoarsely, "Do you want me to wait a second? Should I wait a second?" Somebody muttered an answer and he swallowed, nodded his head, and began to speak.

"Please, don't push little issues, careless esoteric strategies. Try helping me, stat." The screen turned black and the sound ended.

"What does he mean? What is *stat*?" asked Leah

The lieutenant explained, "*Stat* is the first letters of the phrase '*s*ome *t*ime *a*fter *t*his'; it's used to mean, 'as quickly as possible.'" Loser asked that we agree as soon as possible, or, as we say, a-s-a-p, to their demands."

Rabbi Lamdan grimaced. "And I guess you RSVP, *respondez s'il vous plait*, by freeing the prisoners."

"Yes," he said. "That is what we must do."

Leah did not look happy. "What 'little issues' is he worried about?" she asked. "What 'careless esoteric strategies' does he think that you have planned?"

"I don't know. I don't know what he is talking about and that's why I think that he's sending us a message. He's telling us where he is!" He almost shouted it, his frustration evident. "What do you think?"

"I'm sorry," she said. "I can't think of anything."

He stood, looking troubled. "Please, Leah. There must be something in your Torah that can help me. You *always* find a clue from something that you are learning in school. Shall I play the video again? Will that help you? If you knew Loser, you would understand why I feel he is sending a message." He sat down suddenly and sank his head into his hands.

Leah walked nervously around the kitchen as she pondered this new challenge. Myriad thoughts were racing through her mind. And these thoughts were intermingling with one another. She shook her head as she picked up the sheet of paper with the list of possible hideouts and stared at it. Nothing came to mind. She read the sheet of paper carefully, but still did not reach any conclusion.

"Have you written down what Yummy says to you?" she asked. She stopped to correct herself. "I mean, what Loser says to you."

"Sure," was the reply, as McCarthy pulled another sheet of paper out of his briefcase and handed it to Leah. "Here it is!"

Leah stared at the paper. The person who had transcribed Loser's words had written everything he said, including the fact that he asked the kidnappers if they wanted him to wait a second. She looked from one sheet to the other and then back again. She suddenly felt very tense and could not relax. She turned and stared at her father and then at the machzor on the table.

McCarthy seemed tired and anxious. He was so jittery that one of his knees was moving quickly up and down.

"Where does Loser live? Is he married?" asked Leah.

"He lives here in Brooklyn. Rumor has it that he is Jewish. I don't know for sure, but I do know that they got him and transported him to their hideout. I don't know if he is married because although we were friends a long time ago, we didn't keep in touch. He moved up in the world and I didn't."

"But you became a lieutenant ...."

"Loser is one of the top guys in the CIA. We don't socialize anymore."

Leah turned to her parents. "I find the name *Loser* a most interesting name for someone who works for the CIA. Don't you? I know, for example, that Mr. Gartner always gave the kids candy, so the name *Yummy* fit his personality. But why would anyone want to be called *Loser* unless ... unless ...." She paused again. Her eyes lit up. "Unless his name is *Luzer* with a 'z,' short for Elazar and pronounced *Loser* by Polish Jews."

"Are you asking me if he is Jewish?" asked McCarthy. "I don't know. It could be. I told you there were rumors ...."

"So his name may be Luzer Keller," she said. She seemed thoughtful.

"Are you thinking of Eliezer HaKalir?" her father interrupted her thoughts.

"Why not?" asked Leah. "Eliezer HaKalir liked acrostics, and so does Luzer Keller. I wonder if they are related through the generations." She smiled as she spoke.

"What are you talking about?" asked McCarthy.

Leah continued to stare at the two papers she held, one in each hand, and spoke as if she were thinking aloud. "Now that I think of it, when he repeated the words, 'Do you want me to wait a second?' he was handing you another clue." She held out one paper and stared at it. She looked excited about something. "Now I actually see it." She began to *sound* excited. "When he asked about waiting a second, he wanted us to look at the second letter of each word in the sentence he gave you."

McCarthy stared at the copy he held in his hands. "What do you mean?"

Leah was very excited. "Look at the second letter of each word he said. The second letter of the word *Please* is 'l', the second letter of the word *don't* is 'o,' of the word *push* it is 'u,' of *little* it's 'i,' of *issues* it's 's,' and finally, the word *careless* gives us the 'a.' From the second letter of the words 'esoteric strategies, try helping me stat," we find the letters, s,t,r,e,e,t. When we combine them, we have *Louisa Street*! That's one of the streets that you mentioned."

Lieutenant McCarthy's face registered surprise. He was in shock. He needed time to think. He paused and looked at Leah and then he smiled. Then he laughed to himself.

How did this girl figure out the answer to the questions that he posed to her? Then he pulled out his cell phone and called one of the government agents. He spoke quietly to him and then ended the call. He stared back at Leah, saluted her, and turned to go.

"Thank you," he said quietly before leaving the house. "Thank you very much."

A Visitor From The Far East

A Yom Kippur Mystery

Mrs. Lamdan had a surprise waiting for her when she entered the kitchen the morning of Erev Yom Kippur.

"Breakfast is served!" Leah's voice rang out. Mrs. Lamdan stared in astonishment as her daughter turned away from the stove, lifted a skillet from the range, and grinned. "I have for you, dear Mother, a sizzling omelet."

"How thoughtful!" she conceded. "You must have awakened early. I didn't hear any noise from the kitchen this morning!" Rabbi Lamdan was usually the first one in the house to awaken in the morning. He liked to daven at an early minyan. Mrs. Lamdan was usually a "sure" second. But not today! Leah placed the slightly burned omelet on a plate and smiled again.

Her mother eyed Leah carefully and sighed. "I know that it is Erev Yom Kippur, and we usually eat two meals before the fast begins, but an omelet is also a meal and I don't think that I will be able to eat *three* meals before Yom Kippur." She saw the crestfallen look on Leah's face, and stopped herself. "Do you want to share it with me? It should give us both the energy we'll need until lunch." She smiled and invited Leah to join her at the table. "Let's wash, have a small piece of toast, and eat it now."

When Rabbi Lamdan walked in from shul, he smiled at his wife and daughter. "That looks good. Anything left over?" Leah walked over to the oven, opened it, and pulled out another omelet. "I kept it warm while waiting for you," she said. "I think that sometimes, just walking home from shul can create an appetite."

Mrs. Lamdan smiled. She was sipping a cup of coffee. "Leah wanted to prepare a meal for Erev Yom Kippur. So she decided that we need breakfast."

Rabbi Lamdan heaved a sigh. "I wish I could join you but I have to get to yeshivah. I came home just to pick up this sefer that I left on the counter." He showed them the sefer he was holding. "It's all about teshuvah and what we should do before Yom Kippur."

"Yes," said Leah, "I also have a sefer with all the laws of Yom Kippur. I brought it home from school yesterday. We even had a test on it."

Rabbi Lamdan smiled. "Yes," he said in a low tone. "Tomorrow is Yom Hakippurim. It is the fast of the tenth of Tishrei. But the Torah tells us that whoever eats and drinks on the ninth, it is as if he fasted on both the ninth and tenth days of Tishrei. A special quality of the mitzvah of eating on Erev Yom Kippur is that we will be able to complete the fast on the tenth."

"I'm already full," answered Leah. "I feel like the omelet did me in."

Mrs. Lamdan commented, "You'll be all right. You're just not used to such a hearty breakfast. Nor am I, for that matter." She rose from the chair as the phone rang shrilly. "Well," she said, "that's my signal to stop eating. I have lots of things to do today. I have to make sure that all the food that has been prepared for our poor families will be delivered to them on time. Sometimes I tell myself that if I were two people, not just one person, maybe that would help."

Leah smiled back at her mother. "Ima," she said, "if you were two people, you would do double the work!"

The morning passed quickly. Leah took her mother's shopping list and purchased the few additional foods her mother wanted to serve after the long fast. Then she bought herself a pair of Yom Kippur shoes, sandal-like sneakers that were not made of leather and had a Velcro closure that felt comfortable on her feet. The shoe store was packed with many other last-minute shoppers who were looking for comfortable "shoes" for the fast day. Leah's classmate, Sarah Haber, was there too. Sarah glanced at her watch to check the time as she waited on line with Leah to pay for her purchase.

"Did you see a lot of policemen on the avenue today?" she asked Leah.

"Why, do you think that there are more than usual?" Leah shook her head for a moment. Then she stopped and turned back to Sarah. "Come to think of it, I think you're right. When I stepped out of the fruit store before, I was surprised to see two officers eyeing the customers."

"Well, I saw one at the bakery and there is another one across the street right now, walking back and forth." She pointed discreetly and Leah followed the movement of her finger. She too now observed the officer casually walking around and closely observing the various shoppers.

"Something must be going on."

"You think that there is an Erev Yom Kippur mystery? I think that the police look like they are looking for someone or something."

Leah shrugged. She knew that Sarah had that dramatic flair but her powers of observation were pretty good. They left the store and headed toward the next block. A patrol car passed them, and although it was not such an unusual sight, Leah had to agree with her friend that there were quite a number of policemen on duty.

By the time she got home and put away the fresh fruit, the kitchen was bubbling with the delicious aroma of meatballs and pasta. In her house that had become a traditional food for the first meal before the fast. The meatballs were easily digestible, and the family would be able to eat the second meal just before the fast, while the pasta was filling enough to give the strength and energy that would be needed to sustain them during the fast.

The rest of the morning Leah completed some errands before setting the table for their pre-Yom Kippur lunch. Both her father and brother were back early from yeshivah, and her mother had organized the deliveries to the families on her list. They sat down to eat and have a leisurely conversation. They were almost finished when someone rang the doorbell.

Aharon got up to answer the door. When he returned to the table he was accompanied by lieutenant McCarthy, whom he had invited to join the family at the table.

"Hello, everyone," the lieutenant said with a grim smile. "Sorry to disturb you, but I need your help."

Mrs. Lamdan's smile was mirthless. She looked at the lieutenant without a word. She passed him a cup of tea as he sat down and took a little sip.

"What kind of problem do you have on Erev Yom Kippur that can't wait until after the fast?" asked Rabbi Lamdan in a hoarse voice. He was also drinking tea.

Lieutenant McCarthy began to explain. This was serious indeed. The head of a Far Eastern county was coming to visit the United States. He was due to land at JFK Airport in less than four hours. A hero of his country's war of independence, General Aza Zulu was loved by his people and was a staunch friend of the United States. No effort had been spared by our State Department to insure the success of his visit.

"He will spend the evening at a reception at the Museum of Far Eastern Studies and end with a White House dinner and reception the following day," Lieutenant McCarthy said.

"What's the problem?" asked Aharon.

"There is a plot to assassinate him here in New York," sighed McCarthy. "The Secret Service, the FBI, and the local police are working closely with his own security forces to guarantee his safety."

"How can we help?" asked Leah. "We are preparing for Yom Kippur, and I am sure that he will not be visiting any of our shuls."

Lieutenant McCarthy squirmed in his chair. "By coincidence, just the other day we captured a guy who has connections to left-wing terrorist groups. He revealed that he has ties to an organization that has paid a lot of money for someone to shoot our visitor while he is here in the United States."

"What are you planning to do to stop him?" asked Mrs. Lamdan.

"We can't do too much unless we get more facts," he replied grimly. "We know the name of the assassin; he calls himself 'Der Tzvilling,' and we know his modus operandi ... how he operates." He frowned as he rubbed his chin and sipped some more tea.

"'Der Tzvilling?'" asked Rabbi Lamdan. "Is he a twin?"

"He was. His brother was his identical twin, looked just like him, but he was killed a few years ago in some road-side bomb attack in Afghanistan. Most of this terrorist's actions have been against twins. Then, too, he likes to use a double instrument or a two-sided prop against the twin. It could be a double-barreled shotgun, a two-sided knife, or even two similar stones in a slingshot. Once he used the shirt of a baseball team, the Minnesota Twins, to strangle one of our double agents. He is quite inventive."

Leah chuckled. "And this Far Eastern ruler is a twin?" It seemed to be both a question and an answer.

"I'm afraid so." He stared at his cup and tried to cut the conversation short. "An assassin usually has a code name that ties in with the action he plans on doing. We already know the code name he is using in this plot to harm our visitor. For some reason, he is calling this caper 'The Billy the Kid Plot.' I just want to tell you that we don't even know what 'Der Tzvilling' looks like."

"Who is Billy the Kid? Was he a twin?"

"He is an American legend. He was a famous outlaw in New Mexico during the late 1800's. He was a killer and he was killed."

"What's the connection between Billy the Kid and your guest from the Far East?"

"We don't know. We are reviewing the different sites that our guest wants to visit, to see if any of them has any connection to outlaws or the Old West."

"It's Erev Yom Kippur. What can we do? Do you think, perhaps, that the name 'Yom Hakippurim' implies twins?" Aharon chuckled.

"Believe me," snapped McCarthy, "we would grasp at anything." He took some comfort in watching Leah as she quietly listened to their discussion. He felt as if his stomach was twisted in knots, and the tea was doing little good.

"What do you want from us?" she asked "The only twins I know about in our Torah were Yaakov and Esav. And they were very different. Our Rabbis also tell us that Yaakov's sons were born with twin sisters."

"What I would like to do is give you the names of the places that he plans to visit. We will have guards at all these places all the time. However, maybe as you read through the list, something will remind you of twins. If it does, just let me know."

Leah looked at him strangely. "And if I think of something, how will I contact you? I can't use the phone on Yom Kippur."

"I know, I know. But there will be an officer of the law in front of the yeshivah where you go for services. His name is Thomas. If something dawns on you, just walk outside and tell him whatever you are thinking. The rest is up to us."

Rabbi Lamdan glanced at Leah. Her eyes were closed and her hand was on her cheek. Then she opened her eyes and looked at him without saying anything.

McCarthy pulled a list from his jacket pocket. "When he comes in this evening, he will go to the Hilton Hotel. You know of course, that there are many Hilton Hotels that look alike and there are a set of Hilton twin daughters. Do you think that he will be attacked at the hotel? His dinner will be in one of the classical Far Eastern restaurants. I wish we could convince him not to endanger himself, but he feels that he is a general who led his troops in the front lines. He insists that a man brave in war is not a coward in peace. So we must search the rooftops and keep a close watch on the crowd below."

"So, he will be at the Hilton and the restaurant. What else?" She looked flustered.

"Tomorrow morning, he will be at the United Nations. He will deliver an address to the nations of the world. I am quite confident about the protection services over there. Then he is invited with his young son and daughter to the Museum of the Far East and the New York Public Library's division on the Far East. Afterward, they are planning to tour the Bronx Zoo. The goats in their country are white, with long twisted horns. They are the source of cashmere fiber. The general and his family want to know what kind of goats we have. Then they will go to the Empire State Building. Well, that's an American site to see. It just happens that two of their embassy rooms are in the building. Then there will be a formal black-tie dinner later in the evening. Finally, they will leave for Washington and my headache will be gone."

He placed the list on the table and stood up. "I apologize for disturbing you before your holy day, but maybe the combination of your holy day and your brains will be able to help us. We have wanted to catch 'Der Tzvilling' for years and now may be our chance." He exchanged a quick glance with Rabbi Lamdan, nodded to Mrs. Lamdan, and moved away from the table. "Thank you for everything," he said. His eyes darted around the room as he walked quickly out of the kitchen. Aharon escorted him to the door and shook his hand when he left the house.

"Any ideas?" he asked his sister. "What will you do now?"

"I want to shower and relax a little before the fast," she replied.

For the final meal before the fast, the family enjoyed some vegetable soup with chicken. "Don't overeat!" said Mrs. Lamdan. "I don't want you to feel overstuffed and uncomfortable." She placed a bowl of watermelon chunks on the table.

Aharon growled. "Cake would not make me feel overstuffed."

Mrs. Lamdan smiled back at him. "A piece of cold melon is juicy, sweet, and delicious."

Rabbi Lamdan leaned back in his chair. He studied his daughter's face and spoke softly to her. "Next week, you know, is the Yom Tov of Succos. According to the Vilna Gaon, there are two mitzvos that are like twin mitzvos: the mitzvah of living in Eretz Yisrael and the mitzvah of sitting in a succah on Succos. These are both mitzvos that you 'enter into.' Both mitzvos require us to merit the opportunity to perform them. For example, if the Jews sin, Hashem could chas v'shalom expel them from Eretz Yisrael. Similarly, if there is heavy rain, the mitzvah of sitting in the succah is negated. Thus, these two mitzvos are like twins as they show us that we can immerse ourselves in mitzvos. Yom Kippur is a day to concentrate on our tefillos and do teshuvah. I am glad that Lieutenant McCarthy appreciates your powers of observation; however, tomorrow you have other things to concentrate on ...."

Leah nodded. She knew what her father was quietly telling her.

The fast began. The Lamdan family davened in the yeshivah building. When the evening tefillos were completed and they stepped outside, Leah saw an officer sitting in his car and watching the people leave.

Sarah Haber came over to her. "They're afraid of terrorists," she whispered to Leah. "Every shul and yeshivah in the neighborhood has a police car outside."

Bright and early the next morning, Leah and her mother went back to the yeshivah together. Her father and brother had left before them. Before going inside the building, Leah saw the guard pacing back and forth in front of the building, talking on his phone. He seemed agitated. He stopped talking when he saw Leah staring at him and gave her a sympathetic look.

She was glad that the weather was clear. It made it easier to fast. After Shacharis, the reading of the Torah began. Leah concentrated on the Torah reading, which began with the death of the two sons of Aharon the High Priest and then continued with the procedure of the lottery to select the goats for Hashem and for Azazel. Suddenly Leah narrowed her eyes. She sat up quickly and almost missed a sentence of the Kri'ah (Torah reading). The words jumped out at her. She had no evidence, no reason to believe it made sense. But maybe it did. Her face lit up.

When the reader completed the section, she stood up quickly and nodded to her mother. She left the women's section and went outside. Thomas was there. She quickly walked over and tried to speak slowly and deliberately. He swallowed whatever he had been going to say as he looked at her face. She was sheet-white because of the fast, her eyes dark against her pallor. The words seem to jump in her throat and in her head. She wasn't even sure that they came out in the right order. Thomas nodded and got into his car. He was talking on his phone as she returned to the yeshivah.

Later that evening, after the fast was over and the family had eaten their meal, Lieutenant McCarthy came to the door. He was in a good mood.

"Congratulations!" he said. "Thank you! Thank you! We got 'Der Tzvilling.' Your tip paid off!"

"Good!" she laughed. "I'm glad."

"It happened where you suspected it would, at the zoo near the habitat for the Chgnu goats of India. 'Der Tzvilling' somehow got a press pass and entered the roped-off area. He joined our crowd and made his way toward the general. 'Der Tzvilling' moved as close as possible to the general and was poised to run over to him and butt him like a goat, throwing him over the rope into the ravine below. He had an ingenious escape plan also. We found his plans in a hidden pocket in his shirt. You warned us that he would try that. How did you know?"

Leah chuckled. "Today we read our Torah portion for Yom Kippur, all about the lottery of the two he-goats that look exactly alike. One goat is chosen through the lottery as a lofty sacrifice to Hashem on the Altar. The other goat is chosen to be thrown down a mountain. Coincidentally, that goat is referred to as Azazel. It is cast down a mountain to be killed. I was afraid that 'Der Tzvilling' would try to do the same thing to General Aza Zulu. Then I realized why the plot was called 'Billy the Kid'! After all, a kid is a baby goat! I am glad that 'Der Tzvilling's' plot did not succeed! I'm glad that I could help."

The Succos Bracelet

A Succos Mystery

"Here it is, the 12th floor," said Rabbi Lamdan, pointing to the floor map next to the elevator. He smiled pleasantly at his wife as he tried to shake off the drowsiness that had come over him.

"I hope Mr. Nasi has what we want."

"I'm sure he does," answered Mrs. Lamdan cheerfully. "My sister Devorah spoke to him before Yom Tov, and he told her that he has a large selection of bracelets for teenaged girls." She glanced uneasily over her shoulders. "I haven't been in the Diamond Center for such a long time."

Rabbi Lamdan seemed lost in thought. From where she was standing, Mrs. Lamdan could see the bags under his eyes. He was silent a few more seconds and then he said quietly. "It seems silly to me that just because a girl becomes 16, her aunt wants to buy her a piece of jewelry. Why does she need it, and why must we pick it out?"

Mrs. Lamdan smiled gently. "Devorah asked us to choose from several bracelets before Leah makes *her* choice. She wants us to be satisfied also. Since I hope, im yirtzeh Hashem, to phone her today, we may as well let her know that we got Leah the gift that she asked us to pick out. Most young women like jewelry and a beautiful bracelet will always please them. It's a good thing you are free on Chol Hamoed so that we can get it today, since Leah will be visiting her Dodah Devorah on Yom Tov and she will be able to see it right away."

Rabbi Lamdan frowned. "When will Leah arrive?" he asked. And then he added, "What a way to spend the first day of Chol Hamoed!" He looked quite rueful as he thought about how the day was being spent.

"Leah will be here in about 20 minutes, so we have ...." She left her sentence unfinished, nodding in the direction of the man coming toward the elevator.

"Mr. Nasi?" called Rabbi Lamdan.

Mr. Nasi gave a dry brittle cough. His hair was flecked with gray, with salt-and-pepper curly sideburns growing down to join a rounded bushy gray beard and mustache. Very little of his face showed, just a thin, pointed nose, narrow lips, and a pair of dark eyes. He coughed again when he saw the Lamdans standing there.

"Are you Mrs. Goodkin's brother-in-law?" His eyes flashed recognition. The man looked troubled. "Oh! I'm sorry. I must apologize. I forgot to prepare the bracelets." There was a pause. It seemed as if a wave of fatigue swept over him. He peered over, not through, his eyeglasses, and then suddenly his eyes closed and his head sagged momentarily.

Rabbi Lamdan moved forward quickly. "Are you all right?" He looked around for a place for Mr. Nasi to sit a moment but there was no chair in sight.

"Help me outside, please," said Mr. Nasi weakly. "I need fresh air." He forced a smile. "I must eat breakfast and take my pills. There's a succah in front of one of the restaurants on 47th Street." Rabbi Lamdan was holding Mr. Nasi's arm when suddenly, from behind a door, a man dashed forward and grabbed Mr. Nasi's other arm to help him.

"Thank you, Ricky," acknowledged Mr. Nasi. "I feel weak."

Ricky shook his head. "Why do you come if you do not feel well? Isn't today part of your holiday week? Why did you come in to work?" he inquired. Mr. Nasi smiled back.

"Ima?" It was Leah's voice. She had arrived and was concerned when she saw the group in the corridor. "Is something wrong?"

Mrs. Lamdan turned and smiled at her daughter. "Don't worry, dear. It's just that Mr. Nasi does not feel quite well. We will accompany him to the 47th Street succah across the street so that he may eat something. Hopefully, then he'll feel better."

Ricky glared at Leah, and said, with a shake of his head, "Are you the reason Mr. Nasi came to work today, on his holiday? Shame on you! You look like a religious family. I thought religious people don't work or shop today. Why are you here?"

It was Rabbi Lamdan's turn to smile. "Today is one of the intermediate days of the holiday. It is not like the Sabbath, for we may carry and cook and shop for things we will use today or for the last days of the holiday."

Ricky wrinkled his nose. He looked confused. "I remember when Mr. Nasi did not come in to work during the intermediate days."

Mr. Nasi nodded. "I remember those days, too," he laughed. "Times have changed for me. For many years I did not work on Chol Hamoed," he said, "but my brother-in-law, my partner Zalman Ackerman, is an Ashkenazi, who davens in the *Nusach Ashkenaz*. He puts on his tefillin on Chol Hamoed, and then he comes to 47th Street to work. As you probably know, the Ashkenazim follow the ruling of the Mordechai, the Rosh, the Tur, and the Maharil. For them, the letter 'shin' on the tefillin, which numerically means 300, stands for the 300 days in the year that they put on tefillin, excluding the 65 days of Shabbos and the holidays."

"That's true," agreed Rabbi Lamdan. "There are 52 Shabbosim and 13 holidays, bringing the total to 65. Since the 300 days do not include Chol Hamoed as holidays, they feel that tefillin *should* be worn on Chol Hamoed."

"This year Zalman invited lots of company to his house and his succah, so he asked me to do him a favor and come to work instead of him this morning. I daven *Nusach Sefard*. We follow the rulings of Rabbenu Karo of the *Shulchan Aruch*. I do not wear tefillin on Chol Hamoed because in our family Chol Hamoed is considered a minor holiday. On Shabbos we don't wear tefillin, so we don't wear them on Chol Hamoed either. But, for Zalman's sake, I planned on opening up." Then his face clouded. He seemed distressed. His eyes slid away from Leah's glance. "I also wanted to check on the necklace." He seemed very disturbed. "I feel like such a fool."

"Don't upset yourself," said Rabbi Lamdan. "Let's make sure that you eat something first." Mr. Nasi hesitated, and then straightened up. He still held Rabbi Lamdan's arm. He turned and smiled at Ricky. "I think I'll be able to make it to the succah with Mrs. Goodkin's sister, brother-in-law, and their daughter," he said. "Thank you again, Ricky. We won't be gone very long."

Ricky slowly released Mr. Nasi's other arm. He was unable to hide his amazement. Then he shook his head. "It's still a pity that you came. Mr. Ackerman's son was here before you. He wasn't here for a long time. I think he left about a half-hour ago. I know he took something with him, because I saw him carrying a small bag."

"I came later than usual," replied Mr. Nasi sadly.

"It was a long davening," Rabbi Lamdan said. "It doesn't matter whether you daven Ashkenaz or Sefard, the davening is longer on Chol Hamoed." Once outdoors, Mr. Nasi felt better. The Lamdans accompanied him to the succah. Three other people were sitting at one table in the succah. The Lamdans and Mr. Nasi sat at a different table. Mr. Nasi ordered a glass of juice and a bowl of cereal. The food was brought to him almost immediately. He was nodding without saying anything to anyone. Rabbi Lamdan and Leah ordered the same, but Mrs. Lamdan just had a cup of coffee.

"I feel like a fool!" Mr. Nasi suddenly burst out. He had already taken his pills, and his voice already sounded different. He stared into his glass. "I am a fool! How could Zalman do this to me?"

Mrs. Lamdan gasped. Every Tuesday evening she went to a shiur where the participants reviewed the book, *Guard Your Tongue*, an English translation of the writings of the Chofetz Chaim. Mrs. Lamdan tried her best not to listen to *lashon hara*. She set her lips firmly. "Perhaps you do not want to talk about it with us," she suggested hopefully.

Mr. Nasi shook his head and said hoarsely, "I must talk to someone or I shall have a heart attack!" Beyond the far counter someone was cleaning up in the back and waving a dishtowel in his hand.

"What happened?" asked Rabbi Lamdan, clearly surprised.

"Business has not been so good lately. Our partnership has not been an easy one and our sons are very different in nature. Zalman Ackerman's son, Sholom, does not want to go into his father's business. He has been talking about staying in the yeshivah and learning. He has a very good head, they say, and is a serious talmid chacham. This is a new world. Some children just want to 'sit.' My son, Shulem ..." he stammered, suddenly at a loss for words and then, feeling that he had to explain himself, cleared his throat and began again. "Both my sister and I named our sons after our father, *olov hashalom*. My son Shulem just can't 'sit.' He wants to design jewelry. He wants to branch out and expand the business. I don't know what the future holds, but designing jewelry is not my cup of tea. That's for women! It's not for men!" He spoke angrily and forcefully.

Mrs. Lamdan's eyebrows arched. She studied Mr. Nasi carefully as she thought, *Men design clothing. They are cooks and chefs in catering halls, restaurants, and hotels. Why can't they design jewelry as well?*

But Mr. Nasi was still talking, so Mrs. Lamdan strained to listen. There was finally a moment of silence. Mrs. Lamdan pressed the fingers of one hand to her mouth as she looked toward her husband and frowned. Then, in a small voice, she asked, as if she was changing the topic momentarily, "How is Mrs. Ackerman feeling?"

Mr. Nasi groaned and took a deep breath. “My sister, G-d bless her, has not been well. I am sure you know it. The doctors are not sure what is wrong. We pray for her good health, but that’s all we can do now. Zalman is heartbroken. He takes her to so many different doctors! His bills must be enormous. She is my sister. What can I say?” For a moment Mr. Nasi seemed slightly embarrassed.

Rabbi Lamdan frowned. “What happened?” he pressed. “You seem upset with Zalman. What do you think Zalman has done?”

“He has taken my emerald necklace!” Mr. Nasi’s voice changed as he began to explain himself. “This year, Erev Shabbos also happened to be Erev Yom Tov, so I left the necklace on my desk in our office. I covered it with a napkin and forgot to lock it in the safe. And now it is gone! Only Zalman knew that I left it there!”

“Nothing else is missing? Nothing else was taken?”

Mr. Nasi shook his head and looked down at his plate. “I went to the office early to look for a bracelet for you and take care of some other things I wanted to do. And then, I wanted to look again at this new necklace. I couldn’t find it even though I looked everywhere. It’s not on my desk and it’s not in the safe. You heard Ricky say that Sholom was there earlier today and left quickly. His father must have told him about the necklace and its easy accessibility.” He shook his head glumly again.

There was another brief pause and then came the torrent of words. “Friday afternoon, Erev Shabbos, right before we were ready to close the shop, an acquaintance of mine from California came in. His wife had passed away many years ago and now, *nebach*, what a shame, business was bad for him, too. In his prosperous days he had given her a emerald necklace. What a gem! I was the middleman in that deal. Now he has decided to sell it. He knows me, he trusts me, and he knew I would offer him a good price. It is a beautiful, handcrafted necklace. We agreed on a price and I told him that I would give him the money today. We shook hands and he left. As an indication of his trust and faith in me, he left the necklace." He gulped down some water from the glass on the table.

"Zalman and I were ecstatic. What a necklace! What profit we could make! Zalman wanted to contact Kaufman immediately! 'This is big-time jewelry,' Zalman told me. 'Kaufman has a daughter in shidduchim.' When you have a daughter of marriageable age, everyone knows. And to a man like Kaufman, they come with the names of the best boys from the best families."

"Who is Kaufman?" whispered Leah to her mother.

Mr. Nasi heard her. He stroked his beard and looked around carefully. "Kaufman is a rich buyer. When he sees something he likes, he buys. This purchase means a great deal to us. Kaufman would recognize that we have jewels that could interest him, and that is equal to having a very good name in this line."

"Aside from the necklace, was anything else missing?" asked Leah eagerly.

Mr. Nasi frowned. He was a man with a purpose in life, with an ambition to fulfill. He usually wasted little time talking with young girls. But this child was Mrs. Goodkin's niece, and Mrs.Goodkin was a very good client, so he looked at Leah and replied, "Come to think of it, I don't remember seeing my spare tefillin."

Suddenly, one of the men sitting at the table nearby moved back his chair. It scraped against the floor as he spoke quietly into his cell phone. After completing his call, he stood up and walked over to Mr. Nasi, placing an open hand on Mr. Nasi's shoulder.

"A *Gut Moed*," he said with a bountiful smile. "What mazal!" His eyes were twinkling. "You did a good job!" He nodded to Rabbi Lamdan and walked out.

"Do you think he knows something?" Mr. Nasi seemed alarmed.

"Knows what?" asked Rabbi Lamdan.

Mr. Nasi ignored the question. "Zalman and I both studied the necklace, and then I had to step out of the office for a few minutes. I covered the necklace with a napkin, and Zalman went home. Some relatives from his side of the family were coming to him for Yom Tov. Late Sunday night they were scheduled to go back to Toronto, so Zalman wasn't sure whether he could open the business in the morning. That's why we agreed that I would come in. As I said, I rarely come to work during Chol Hamoed. On the first day of Yom Tov, I saw him walking along with his relatives on Fifteenth Avenue. The next day, I heard from someone in shul that one of the relatives caught a virus and had a fever. Who knows if they've gone back to Toronto yet."

"And all this time, over Shabbos and Yom Tov, the emerald necklace remained on your desk in your office?" *What carelessness!* Mrs. Lamdan mused. "Why didn't you put it in your safe before you left the office?"

Mr. Nasi looked uncomfortable. "Please don't think that I am such a careless individual. When I returned to the office, Zalman had already gone home, and my wife called. She was desperate! She needed some ingredient for something she was cooking and she could not leave the house or send any of the children for it. Shulem was not home either. You know how women are when they're in the middle of a recipe, in the kitchen preparing for Shabbos." He suddenly looked embarrassed and uncomfortable as he glanced at Mrs. Lamdan. "What I mean to say is ...," he sputtered an apology.

"Never mind," said Mrs. Lamdan. "I am not interested in your view on women. What did you do?"

"I checked the office. The safe was locked. I unplugged the hot-water kettle. I checked that everything else was in place, the extra pair of tefillin was on the shelf, and I locked the door. I didn't remember the necklace because it was hidden under the napkin." He sighed. "Out of sight, out of mind," he grumbled half to himself.

Leah perked up. "Why do you have spare tefillin on the shelf?" she asked. She smiled. "That almost sounds like having a spare tire in the car."

"It is a spare," acknowledged Mr. Nasi. "There have been times when we were so busy that Zalman and I would daven in a shtiebel a few blocks away from our business. We would actually sleep here overnight and then in the morning we needed our tefillin to daven. So we always kept a spare pair here."

"Fine," interrupted Rabbi Lamdan. He was becoming impatient. "So you locked up and left the necklace on your desk under the napkin. Then what?"

Mr. Nasi frowned. "I had a worrisome Shabbos and Yom Tov."

"Did you tell Mr. Ackerman about it?"

"And ruin his Yom Tov, too?" Mr. Nasi looked horrified. "How could I do that to Zalman? He has enough problems to contend with. My wife warned me not to say anything to him, but now, look at what's happened — Zalman must have taken the necklace!"

"You mean his son, Sholom," corrected Rabbi Lamdan.

Mr. Nasi shook his head. "Sholom is a good boy. I told you that he is also a talmid chacham .... I know what you're thinking. But he is not the type of young man to do such a thing if he knew it was *assur*, to do so. Maybe his father asked him to take it and Sholom listened to his father. He respects his father, not like my Shulem. At the Yom Tov table, Shulem complained that I harass him too much. When I told him not to anger me because I was already concerned about the emerald necklace, he laughed at me. Is that what I worried about on Shabbos? He would not worry about it. After all, Hashem watches everything, even an emerald necklace. And then, he had the chutzpah to ask me if I would give the necklace to him for a day or two, to redesign it. 'You know,' he said to me, 'just like clothing must be updated and styles change, so must jewelry. Stylish young ladies would not want to wear the expensive clothes they wore two years ago, so why would one of them want a necklace from 20 or 30 years ago!' The fool! My son Shulem is a fool! He wants to design jewelry! Meanwhile, Zalman has taken the jewel."

Leah mentally reviewed the facts. "Where is Shulem now?" she asked.

"Who knows? I decided to come in early today. I asked Shulem to come with me. The silly boy declined. He said that he had to get up very early to meet one of his friends. He was out of the house even before I left."

A tall man entered the succah. He waved to Mr. Nasi and walked over to him. "*Gut Moed*," he said. "That was good!" and then he waved to the man still sitting at the next table and walked over to him.

Leah glanced sidelong at her mother. She bit her lower lip and shook her head.

"How can I afford to pay for that necklace?" lamented Mr. Nasi. "I must pay my friend from California. I dare not tell him what has happened. Our reputation as honest brokers must remain untarnished."

Leah shook her head. "Religious men put on tefillin from the time they become Bar Mitzvah. Only last week, I read somewhere how to put the *tefillin shel yad* correctly on the arm and hand. The leather is wound three times around the upper arm, forming the Hebrew letter 'shin.' Then it is wrapped seven times down the forearm, across the palm, and around the fingers in such a way as to spell out two more letters, 'dalet' and 'yod,' forming one of Hashem's names. While the tefillin are wrapped, prayers are said. I assume that someone religious enough to put on tefillin daily would be ethical enough not to steal. Yet you are accusing your brother-in law and his son, your nephew, of committing such a terrible act."

It was apparent to Leah that Mr. Nasi was emotionally exhausted. That could be the only excuse for him to be lambasting his son and speaking negatively about him. "Why do you accuse your son of being a fool?" she asked aloud. "He wants to expand your business. He seems to have some interesting and innovative ideas, and you call him a fool? My teacher, Rebbetzin Zimmerman, always tells us that a bitter person thinks only bitter things. A sad person thinks sad thoughts. For Jews there is a mitzvah to be happy, especially when performing mitzvos. When you learn Torah, you must be happy so that you will see the good in people," she exclaimed.

Leah then had a thoughtful look on her face. She seemed ready to say something else, but she hesitated as she tried to formulate her words. Everyone waited and watched her and then she began. "Mr. Nasi ...", her voice trailed off helplessly. Then she began again. "You don't have to worry about Mr. Kaufman. I have a feeling that within the hour, you will regret everything you said about all the members of your family — your son, your nephew, and your brother-in-law. Zalman Ackerman's son, Sholom, is a fine and kind Torah scholar. Your son, Shulem, will have outdone you at your craft. I wish you Mazal and Berachah and a *Gut Moed*."

"What?" shouted Mr. Nasi. "What do you know? What do you mean?"

"It is obvious that Zalman's son Sholom came to the office early. I think he picked up the spare tefillin to bring home to your guest. When he returns to your office later, he will probably be carrying the tefillin. He and his father did not know before Shabbos that you left the emerald necklace on your desk, covered by a napkin. No! Sholom only came for the tefillin, because, as we said before, Ashkenazim put on tefillin on Chol Hamoed and Mr. Ackerman's guest didn't leave because he wasn't feeling well. He probably did not bring his own tefillin with him to New York because, as you said, he expected to return to Toronto Sunday night, after Yom Tov. He needed tefillin this morning."

"So who took the necklace?" Mr. Nasi could not contain himself. "Are you accusing my Shulem?"

"Not at all!" Leah leaned back in her chair. "It is true that your son Shulem knew about the necklace that you left on your desk. I wouldn't be surprised if he was at your office this morning even earlier than Ricky. I think he may have re-designed the necklace according to Mr. Kaufman's daughter's taste and the word on the street is that Mr. Kaufman is very pleased!"

Mr. Nasi looked bewildered. He looked from Rabbi Lamdan to Mrs. Lamdan and back to Leah. Leah made him nervous. His heart seemed to race out of control. He gave Leah a skeptical look.

Leah responded with a happy grin. "That's why these two men approached you with a 'Mazal Tov.' They have their cell phones with them, and on 47th Street I am sure that people know that your son re-designed an emerald necklace for Miss Kaufman, and Mr. Kaufman loved it! You did a good job!"

Mr. Nasi took in every word that Leah said. He pounded his fist on the table. "Come," he ordered. "Come back to my office. If you are right, I will not charge your aunt for the bracelet and your mother can choose a nice piece of jewelry also. If you are right, then I will learn to change my attitude toward my family and toward others as well. If you are right, I will donate four times *chai*, four times $18, to any *tzedakah* you want. If ...."

And Leah was right!

A Winter Spy

A Chanukah Story

The phone rang shrilly. Leah Lamdan looked up from the book she was reading while sprawled on the carpet in the living room.

"Are you picking it up?" she asked her brother Aharon, who was reviewing some English homework. He stretched and raised his arms over his head.

"I think Ima is picking it up in the kitchen," he replied.

They heard Mrs. Lamdan lift the receiver and say, "Hello?" and then there was silence. Aharon got up quickly as Leah scrambled behind him.

"Ima? Is everything all right?" Instinctively they ran into the kitchen, then stopped and stared. Mrs. Lamdan was grinning from ear to ear. "We won!" she said. Her eyes fluttered, then widened as she shot a hand out to grip Leah's arm. "We won!" she repeated again. "We won the trip to Israel. Your father and I won." She turned and looked into Aharon's eyes. "You'll be able to stay in the yeshivah dormitory for Chanukah. You've been pleading with us for the chance to stay in the dorm. Well, Abba and I will be going to Eretz Yisrael for Chanukah!"

"How could you have made all these arrangements already?" Leah asked in amazement. "You just found out that you won and you already have plans!"

Through the kitchen window, they could see snow falling in thin slick flakes as Mrs. Lamdan gleefully continued, "We made contingency plans beforehand and decided that if we won, we would go Eretz Yisrael for Chanukah. Aharon can stay in the dorm, and you, Leah," she grinned again, "had already decided to join your class for Chanukah in the Catskills."

Many of the girls in Leah's class in Bais Malkah had been involved in a special tzedakah project for the school. When their project was completed, the school was contacted by a national organization that wanted to reward the girls who were so active in chessed. A house in the Catskill Mountains was rented for the week of Chanukah and the girls who had participated in the project, as well as their morah and her family, were invited to spend the week in a mansion that had 25 rooms, including 14 bedrooms. Separate stairwells led to seven bedrooms on each side of the house. The girls would double or triple up in their rooms in one wing, while Rabbi and Rebbetzin Zimmerman, their children, the cook and her family, and the caretaker would all have rooms in the other wing of the house.

A kosher hotel nearby was booked for the entire week for a family simchah. That meant that Rabbi Zimmerman and his sons would be able to daven with a minyan.

Chanukah drew near during the snowiest December in years. The streets were blanketed with snow and the change in the weather was a bit startling. But the excitement in the Lamdan household was palpable. The day before they departed, Mrs. Lamdan was bustling around the kitchen preparing certain things for each of her children, doing the laundry, packing their suitcases, and writing numerous lists with their itinerary and phone numbers.

Rabbi Lamdan seemed excited but unfazed by it all. He drove Aharon to the dormitory. Aharon took along the menorah he had received as a Bar Mitzvah present from his grandparents. The wisdom of taking a silver menorah had been debated for several days, but the family was so enthusiastic about having won the main prize that Rabbi Lamdan, who was usually a bit more cautious, told his son to enjoy the mitzvah of lighting his beautiful menorah. Leah had also packed a menorah, but hers was not silver.

There are two Yom Tov mitzvos we look at that are referred to as the "Re'Esem Mitzvos." "You shall see the kos of wine on Pesach and you shall see the menorah shining forth from your window or entrance." To fulfill the Re'Esem of the wine, we lift our wineglasses at the Pesach Seder and we recite the berachah that we became free men. For the mitzvah of the menorah, we place our menorahs where all can see them, because Hashem helped us win against our enemies.

Her parents drove Leah to the bus that would take her and her excited classmates to the mountains. Not all the girls were going. Out of the class of 24 girls, only eight would be going on the bus. Some girls would come up in the middle of the week and nearly all the rest would join them for Shabbos. Leah hugged her parents as goose pimples covered her arms under her warm jacket. This would be her first Chanukah away from home. Her mother handed her a phone number.

"This is Lieutenant McCarthy's number. He asked me to give it to you. Just in case ... just in case ...."

Leah simply smiled.

Rabbi and Rebbetzin Zimmerman greeted each parent. They, too, had an itinerary and showed it to the Lamdans. "It is a very big, warm house. We will have many activities inside and outside. We will try to make their Chanukah a beautiful one and their Shabbos Chanukah 'enlightening.'"

The girls boarded the bus and waved to their parents and families. They were on their way at last! It would take almost four hours to reach the mansion. The eight friends were Chanah from Israel, Devorah from Los Angeles, the twins Sarah and Yocheved, Estee who liked to spell her name with two 'e's, Shifra the class reader, and Rochel who loved math. And, of course, there was Leah.

The Zimmermans traveled in their car, following the bus as the girls began to sing Chanukah songs. It was cold outside and the windows were closed. They could see their breath as the beautiful songs filled the air. But after more than three hours of driving, they were tired, and most of them closed their eyes and let the whoosh of the tires lull them to a half-sleep.

The honking sound of the bus horn woke them. Leah stood up and looked out the window. Two police cars were blocking the road, their flashing lights spinning. They signaled to Moishe, the driver, to stop. Two officers walked over to the bus. The driver opened the door to let them in, but they told him to come outside. He was not pleased as he rose from his seat, moved heavily down the steps, and closed the door behind him. By that time, Rabbi and Rebbetzin Zimmerman had reached the side of the bus and joined the driver at the side of the road.

"What is it? What's wrong?" asked Shifra. "Why have we stopped?"

Leah moved toward the front of the bus. "The Zimmermans seem to be arguing with the police," she announced. "I don't understand why." She quietly opened the door of the bus to listen to the conversation.

"Sorry, we can't let you pass. I see your letter, but I am not permitted to let you continue on this road. The government has invited many foreign ministers to visit us this week and discuss important issues. We have been ordered to put up a roadblock and block all unauthorized vehicles. I don't care what kind of letter you have from a charity. You don't have official authorization to be up here, and I cannot permit you to go farther."

The driver was almost in tears. His English was not as good as his Russian and he was afraid to answer any questions. He was terrified that he would be sent back to Russia. He grew confused and disoriented. Rabbi and Rebbetzin Zimmerman asked to speak to someone in charge. The officer contacted his superiors via his car radio and explained the situation to them.

It had suddenly turned very cold. An icy wind blew into their faces. The icicles hanging on the trees caused the branches to droop. Suddenly they heard a siren. Another police car hurtled down the road. It stopped right in front of the bus and a heavyset man stepped out into the cold. He wheezed heavily, coughed harshly, and turned to another officer following behind him. Leah gasped. The second officer was Lieutenant McCarthy! What was he doing up here in the Catskills?

Leah heard the first officer mutter between coughing fits, "What is going on here, Sergeant? No outsiders are allowed in this area." He leaned against the Zimmermans' car and nodded curtly. He glared at them disapprovingly.

"Madame. Sir. I wish to inform you that the government of the United States of America has declared the right of eminent domain in this territory. " His lips twitched. Was it the cold or was it anger at the audacity of this small group of people wishing to defy him? He suddenly whirled and pointed his finger at the bus and Leah. He shouted at her, "Young lady, don't you get off the bus!"

Leah froze with shock as all eyes turned toward her.

"Leah? Leah Lamdan?" Lieutenant McCarthy moved stiffly forward.

"Who is this? You know this kid?" the officer looked at McCarthy.

McCarthy looked embarrassed. "These kids live in my Brooklyn precinct. I know the parents of some of these girls," he said in a low voice.

Moishe re-entered the bus to try to turn it around but the engine coughed and wouldn't start. He waited a bit and tried again. He gave a short laugh and tossed his head in annoyance. He tried again but the engine did not respond. He held up both hands in frustration.

Then another car, complete with shrieking siren, arrived. A chauffeur stepped out, hurried to the passenger door, and opened it. Leah recalled an expression Lieutenant McCarthy had once used to describe an important politician who dressed to impress the people. McCarthy referred to him as "The Wardrobe." "The Wardrobe" had finally been sent to prison on a slew of charges of corruption.

As this "Wardrobe" got out of the car in his fur-lined coat, he haughtily inspected everyone present.

"Minister Oswego," the first officer saluted, then moved toward him. "Is everything all right?"

"Who are these people? Why are they here? We need solitude, not trespassers." He waggled his hand and turned his face sideways, "away from the rabble."

Rabbi Zimmerman coughed. There was color back in his face and the shadows under his eyes seemed to be gone. "We have been invited by the Bikur Cholim Organization to stay at North Woods Manor for the week. We were not told that any problems would arise because of our visit."

The minister sniffed. He closed his eyes and breathed in the cold air as if he were savoring some pleasant aroma. Then he opened his eyes again and smiled. "Yes. Yes. I vaguely remember hearing something about a group of religious girls who won some contest. The winners have a week here in the mountains. Too bad. We will be here, too. And if the ministers are here, then you cannot be! Our multinational discussions must remain secret. Too many times, our most private conversations have been revealed. We have been promised an absolute block on any microphones, tapes, or surveillance equipment." He stood tall, confident in his influence over everyone.

Moishe coughed and tried to clear his throat as he stumbled down the steps of the bus. "I'm sorry, Kommisar," he said. "The bus doesn't start ...."

The officer who seemed to be in command looked angrily at McCarthy. "Get someone to start it!"

"Of course," was the reply. "It is only 8 o'clock in the evening. I am sure we can rouse ...."

"Never mind, never mind," said the minister. "They are only innocent students. I am sure that they will cause us no harm. But once they are on the property of the manor, they must remain there." He turned around, got into his car, and nodded to the driver. The chauffeur drove away as quickly as he had come.

McCarthy, the other officer, and the two troopers stood quietly in the cold. Moishe climbed back into the bus and held the steering wheel.

"Yaaleh v'yavo," shouted the twins.

"Yaaleh v'yavo," chorused the other girls.

The engine suddenly jumped to life with a roar and the bus started to move. Rabbi and Rebbetzin Zimmerman ran back to their car and happily followed the bus to North Woods Manor.

It was nearly 9 p.m. when they arrived, and the girls unloaded their luggage and entered the mansion. They had never seen a house like it. "It reminds me of Cinderella's castle when she married the prince," said Estee.

There were two circular staircases with exquisite paintings all around the walls. The central chandelier glowed with iridescent bulbs shaped like flames. The living room had ten couches and divans in addition to enormous armchairs and chaise lounges.

"The first thing we must do is to light our Chanukah licht. After we light the menorahs, you will each contact your parents and let them know that we have arrived safely. It's been a very long trip and the cook has a delicious meal prepared for you. I am driving over to the hotel nearby and I hope I will have a minyan."

The girls did as they were told and they savored the tasty dinner that had been prepared. Rebbetzin Zimmerman joined them and then unpacked her things and put her children to bed. Everyone was exhausted. They chose their rooms and went to sleep. Leah was awakened once in the middle of the night by a buzzing sound.

She got up and looked outside the window. *Oh, well!* she thought to herself. *That must be one of the sounds of the country.*

The next morning after davening and breakfast, the girls decided to make snowmen. Each girl made her own and decorated the figures with twigs and scarves. They laughed together and rolled in the snow. Rochel found a garbage-can lid that they used as a sled, climbing up a small hill and sliding down. Their shouts of laughter and joy could be heard all over the property.

To their surprise, Lieutenant McCarthy came over. He spoke briefly to Rabbi Zimmerman, who called the girls inside. "The ministers discuss important matters all day, till midnight. Afterward they confer privately with each other to negotiate some more. You are not allowed to make too much noise, since it disturbs the conference members, who rest early in the day."

In the afternoon they listened to tapes and read. Shifra was very artistic and drew a picture of the landscape. Estee, Rochel, and Devorah went into the kitchen and helped the cook prepare supper and make latkes. The twins, Yocheved and Sarah, prepared a skit as their night activity. Leah had been asked to deliver a shiur on Chanukah and she was busily reviewing some material she found in one of the bookcases.

After lighting their menorahs for the second night, the girls ate and played some games. They heard the sound of sirens not too far away, and Leah, who had brought along a pair of binoculars (Aharon had once told her that since she was involved in mysteries, she should always be equipped with binoculars and a magnifying glass), looked out the window to see what was happening. But it was too dark to see anything. Each girl took a turn looking through the binoculars, but the trees and snowmen blocked their view.

Once she was back in her room, Leah used her binoculars again. The moon was full. She admired their snowmen all standing in a row not far from her window. The wind was blowing against the snowmen whose scarves waved to and fro in the cold. They reminded her of a song about soldiers standing in a row. It was oddly comforting to see something you had made standing stalwart, eight hearty snowmen standing in a row. Each girl had placed a cup holding a candle made of snow in her snowman's hand. Every day, as long as the snowmen would last, the friends intended to place a red scrap of paper on each snow candle and pretend that it represented a Chanukah light ... another night ... of Chanukah. She finally went to sleep.

She woke up suddenly. She thought she heard something. She looked at her watch; it was 2 o'clock in the morning! She rose and grabbed her binoculars in order to look out the window again. The eight snowmen were still standing in a row. But approximately 100 feet away, closer to the other estate, stood a lone snowman all by itself. Her eyes almost popped out of their sockets. Was it possible? Where had this other snowman come from? She had heard of people being snow blind, but she could see clearly. She counted again. She counted nine! Perhaps one of the girls had made an extra snowman as a shamesh for their eight-snowmen menorah, all in a row. She shrugged. She started to call out to one of her friends but changed her mind. It was, after all, 2 o'clock in the morning. She was tired. It had been a long day and she went back to sleep.

After breakfast the next morning, the girls went outside. The eight snowmen were still lined up; it was so cold that they had hardly melted. The ninth snowman that Leah thought she had seen was not there. She decided that she had been very tired and she must have been mistaken.

That night, after lights out, Leah closed her eyes but couldn't sleep. She got up, pulled out her binoculars, and looked at the eight snow shapes all in a row. Yes, she confirmed, there were only eight.

In the middle of the night, again around 2 o'clock in the morning, she was awakened by a buzzing sound. She got up, took her binoculars, and looked out. There it was. The lone snowman was standing silently at a distance from the other eight. Nothing moved. It seemed to be cold, but there was no wind. Leah didn't want to stand and stare, but there was too much curiosity in her to refuse. She smiled in the dark and made her plans for the next day. She waited until early in the morning. After davening, she dressed herself warmly and ran outdoors. She let out a sigh as she counted the eight white snowmen standing in a row, like a menorah waiting to be lit. She stared at each one of them. Chanah's menorah was leaning over slightly. The rays of the sun beamed down and a little of the snow had melted to one side. She wandered over to the next one; was it Estee's? One of the coal eyes had fallen out and the face looked a little strange. She stared at the ground beneath the snowmen; it was clean and white, unmarked by footprints. The girls had not touched their snowmen since they had worked on them the previous day, and the wind had erased their footprints. She smiled to herself.

It wasn't her style, it wasn't her way, but there were times, she thought, you just went with the moment. She counted out 100 paces as she walked and found herself stranding in front of a barbed-wire fence. She leaned over slightly next to the fence and looked at the ground. The snow was smooth, white, and clean. But this snow looked as if the top layer had been brushed carefully with a whisk broom.

She raised her fingers to her lips as she thought she heard a funny buzzing sound. And then she realized that her cell phone was vibrating. She had turned it off for the night and forgotten to turn the ringer back on. She quickly dug her hand into her pocket and pulled it out. It was so cold outside that her teeth began to chatter. "Abba," she said. "Hi!"

"Leah, Leah, is everything all right?" He sounded worried and anxious.

Her mother was obviously standing next to him; she took the phone and called out, "Are you sure everything is all right? The newspapers here in Israel have written about the Ministers' Summit near the mansion where you are staying. A spy keeps revealing what the ministers are talking about. It seems as if the whole world is in an uproar about it."

"I'm fine, Ima," Leah answered. "The conference is going on without us! Please don't worry." Leah began to walk around so that she would not freeze to the spot during the conversation with her parents.

"I am so sorry that we are not together for Chanukah, but Abba and I are warm and comfortable here in Jerusalem." Then her voice changed its tone. Leah recognized the serious expression straining her mother's voice. "Leah, maybe you should contact Lieutenant McCarthy and tell him where you are. He knows you're up in the mountains. I told him that we were going away for Chanukah and I would appreciate an extra eye watching our house. He told me that he was going away also. I had to laugh when he told us that he would not be far from you. Stay away from mysteries and enjoy yourself, darling. Enjoy your Chanukah with your friends."

Leah arched her brows and speculated about her conversation with her parents. She clenched her jaw tightly into a stern expression. She felt so far away from home and yet mysteries continued to find her. She scrambled back to her room and stood by the window, hesitating. Then she looked up Lieutenant McCarthy's cell phone number and called him. They had spoken for a few minutes when the buzzer sounded for breakfast. It was time to prepare for the new day. A smile curved her lips. Tomorrow the rest of the girls would be coming for Shabbos and this mystery would be put out of her mind.

Around 3 o'clock in the morning, she heard a variety of sounds coming from outside. Leah got up quickly and peered out the bedroom window. Her eyes narrowed as she folded her arms and watched the police officers milling about outside. Spotlights were flashing around the snowmen. Most of the lights were trained on the lone snowman a hundred feet away. Her cell phone began to ring. Leah relaxed as she answered the phone and heard Lieutenant McCarthy's voice.

"I saw you standing by your window, so I knew that you were awake," he said. "Your suspicions were correct. Inside that snowman was a man operating an electronic eavesdropping system. It uses a laser beam that can pick up the vibrations caused by voices inside a room. In Washington some of our offices have special curtains that block this eavesdropping device."

Leah listened and frowned. "But the ninth snowman wasn't there all the time," she said. "Why was it gone in the morning? Where did it go?"

"They were afraid to keep the snowman out all day lest someone become suspicious. But late at night they set up the snowman not far from your snowmen and tested the equipment. Then they moved the snowman closer to the ministers' window. No one suspected anything because they knew that there were kids around — you girls— and that you had made snowmen.

"In the morning everyone thought that the ninth snowman they had seen was just part of your group. They didn't suspect that there was a fake snowman planted near the Ministers' Summit. After listening in on the meetings and private discussions, the spy returned to the spot near the fence, to shut down his equipment and prepare what he needed for the next day. That's why early in the morning, you saw the ninth snowman. He had just returned from his eavesdropping mission."

Lieutenant McCarthy's lips tightened as he began to feel the cold. "I just think that it is admirable that you realized there was an extra snowman," he added.

Leah's eyes widened as she pursed her lips and shook her head. "We are eight girls. Each of us made her own snowman. There could be only eight, not nine, because Chanukah is an eight-day holiday."

A Healthy Mystery

A Tu B'Shevat Mystery

Mrs. Lamdan's dear friend Yehudis had lost a great deal of weight, motivated by potential health issues. A new, healthful diet was one her best way to combating overweight. The clock read just shy of 8:30 in the morning when she rang the doorbell of the Lamdan house and stepped over the threshold as soon as Mrs. Lamdan answered.

Yehudis moved across the living room into the kitchen and without fanfare opened the refrigerator door. "Here it is," she announced as she placed a large container on the top shelf. "I have for you this delicious health salad I made that will provide you with the energy boost you need."

"Is that supposed to be for Tu B'Shevat?" Mrs. Lamdan asked. "Aharon's yeshivah has a brochure of items to order for the festive occasion." Tu B'Shevat is a delicious holiday. Families partake of many kinds of fruit, especially fruit from Eretz Yisrael. Figs, dates, and pomegranates are often enjoyed during the month of Shevat. Tu B'Shevat marks the beginning of the new year for fruit. It may be the beginning of the budding or the beginning of the ripening, but we celebrate it as a festival. One of the ways Mrs. Lamdan celebrated Tu B'Shevat was by sending her children's rebbeim and teachers a gift of fruit to thank them for teaching and guiding her children.

Yehudis smiled. "Why is it called Too B'Shevat. Shouldn't it be called Shevat, Too?"

Leah's mother stared back at her friend, not sure if she was joking. Yehudis was a chozeres biteshuvah, who had become religious nearly seven years earlier. Yehudis sometimes still felt unsure of herself when it came to matters of religion, and did not hesitate to ask about issues that were unclear to her.

"It is called 'Tu' because in Hebrew those two letters, 'tes' and 'vav,' stand for the numbers 9 and 6, which equal 15," Mrs. Lamdan explained. "The holiday takes place on the 15th of the month of Shevat. It's the New Year of the Trees. In fact, our Rabbis tell us that if a congregation wishes to declare a fast of BeHab, when people fast on the second day of the week, the fifth day, and the following second day again — that is, Monday, Thursday, and Monday — the fast would have to be postponed to avoid falling on Tu B'Shevat."

Mrs. Lamdan sighed wearily as she sniffled into some tissues and blew her nose. Every year in honor of Tu B'Shevat Mrs. Lamdan made a special jelly from the esrog that had been used on Succos, and that jelly was eaten on Tu B'Shevat. But, at this moment, Mrs. Lamdan was not thinking about the jelly. She dropped onto a chair and said, "I have a bad cold. My energy level is at its lowest.

And just listen to my schedule! Several other parents and I have a meeting today at 9:30 with Rabbi Eisenberg, the principal of Bais Malkah High. It's in regard to some extra-curricular program the school is planning for the upcoming year. At noon, I'm supposed to meet Sora Gitty at the Bikur Cholim office. We have scheduled an important discussion about our delivery to one of the hospitals. And finally, at 3 o'clock, I promised to substitute in the afternoon in the Rayim Ahuvim pre-school. Morah Sarah Leah has an appointment that she can't reschedule.

"Energy boost, you say? I have a cold that is draining both my sinuses and my energy. What do you have for that?" She smiled weakly and looked baffled. "Do you also want to hear my schedule for this evening? Baruch Hashem, we have been invited to a vort and a chasunah. Do you think that it will snow? That would be the last straw!"

"Sarah," said her friend, "do me a favor. Eat the salad and go back to sleep. I will call all these places and cancel your meetings. You must take care of yourself before caring for others and their concerns."

Sarah Lamdan smiled. "I was hoping that you would offer to go to the meeting with Rabbi Eisenberg instead of me. We just want to show him that we are a united parent body."

Yehudis gave her a wary look and hastily said that no, of course it wasn't possible. She did not have children in the school, and would not be able to offer any input at the meeting.

The doorbell rang again and Yehudis offered to see who was at the door. She came back with Leah.

"I forgot my key," the girl explained, "and I was afraid that you wouldn't be home when I got back. I know you have a very busy schedule today."

Mrs. Lamdan sighed. She not only had a headache, but definitely a bad headache. Leah looked at her mother and frowned. "Do you want me to stay home while you rest? I can always go back later."

"That's a wonderful idea," Yehudis remarked. "And I will be on my way, too. Just make sure that your mother eats this healthy salad, because I think that that is what she really needs." With that comment and a delighted look, she waved and left the house.

Mrs. Lamdan closed her eyes. "Sometimes I wish that everyone had the independence and dignity and ability to do what our Torah conscience tells us to do. If that were the case, I think I would lose my headaches."

Leah smiled and walked over to the refrigerator. "What kind of salad did she make?" she asked.

"I call it her karpas salad. It includes carrots, radishes, potatoes, and celery and sometimes nuts and lettuce. I guess the nuts make it suitable for Tu B'Shevat. It is quite healthful but the chewing will make my headache worse. Those four vegetables have become a mnemonic based on the karpas that we eat at our Pesach Seder."

Leah laughed. "What's that word? I don't remember hearing that before. How do you spell it? Do you know of any other noo — what...?" but she couldn't remember the word.

Mrs. Lamdan smiled. She had been a high-school English teacher for many years. "The word is mnemonic, m-n-e-m-o-n-i-c. You don't pronounce the first 'm.' It's a Greek word that means 'an aid to the memory.' It helps you memorize certain words or phrases, such as the planets in the sky. I remember learning their names by memorizing this sentence, 'My Very Educated Mother Just Served Us Nine Pizzas.' Each letter stood for a planet ...

Mercury, Venus, Earth, Mars, Jupiter, Saturn, Uranus, Neptune, and Pluto. Recently, scientists decided that Pluto is not a planet, so perhaps the sentence has been changed because the last word would not be included."

Leah smiled thoughtfully. "We once had to study the names of the presidents of the United States. One of the girls in class actually wrote a mnemonic." She pronounced the word slowly so that she would be able to remember it. "'Washington and Jefferson Made Many a Joke' ... that stands for Washington, Adams, Jefferson, Madison, Monroe, Adams, and Jackson."

Just then, she was interrupted by the ringing of the bell.

"No visitors for me," said her mother. "I am going to eat a little salad and then lie down."

Leah answered the door to discover Lieutenant McCarthy standing nervously in front of the house.

"Ah, Leah!" he said. His eyes shone gratefully.

"Hi, Lieutenant! How are you today?" asked Leah.

"Why aren't you in school yet?" he questioned. "Do you need a lift?" He stepped back and stood waiting for an answer.

Leah stared at him and shook her head. "My mother isn't feeling well, so I probably will be home this morning," she told him. "But thanks for the offer."

"Nothing serious, I hope."

"Bad cold," was the reply. "I hope she's resting."

McCarthy sat down on the stoop in front of the house and smiled. "I understand. But I must talk to you about something important. Maybe we can talk outside."

"Sure," she answered. "What's up?"

He passed her some papers and let her look at them. He waited for her to finish reading. "I don't understand this at all," she said. "You have given me one sheet of paper with the names and occupations of different individuals. Mr. Bert Myles is a geography teacher in the local high school. Mrs. Anna Ryder is a school secretary. Dr. Clark Barton is a doctor, and Mr. Anthony Bates is a lawyer. I don't know these people, so why are you giving me their names and occupations? And then you gave me a second sheet ...."

He bit his lip but not because of the cold. "There was a robbery yesterday at a museum in Brooklyn, in my very own precinct. A famous painting was stolen. We suspect that one of these four individuals committed the crime."

"How can I help if I don't even know them?"

"The local newspaper hasn't revealed all the information. The minute the alarm went off we were on our way. We must have just missed the thief. He must have just grabbed the painting and run away. He probably wore gloves, as there were no fingerprints. Anyway, he dropped something. We found it on the floor near a spot where the painting used to hang. It is a piece of paper with two sentences on it. They make no sense to us, but maybe, just maybe, you'll understand them."

Leah frowned. This really seemed ridiculous. *How did the lieutenant come up with such things?* she thought.

"Is this the paper with the sentence on it?"

"Yes!" He nodded very quickly. "We believe that the thief dropped this paper as he reached up to grab the painting."

Leah studied the piece of paper. It had been folded over ever so tightly, pleated like an accordion. She opened it carefully. There were two sentences. One said, "Eat An Aspirin After A Night Snack." The other said, "I Am A Person."

She read it aloud. "'Eat An Aspirin After A Night Snack.'" She frowned. "'I Am A Person.'" She turned the paper around. “The world is full of crazy people,” she said.

“Do you think the paper belongs to the doctor because he deals with aspirin?” asked the lieutenant. “Maybe this paper belongs to the school secretary because she doles out aspirin to students who have headaches. A lawyer or even a teacher would be the kind of person to announce, ‘I am a person.’ I guess if we think long enough, something will come to mind.”

Leah sat down on one of the steps in front of the house. She was trying to think of something that was teasing her memory when Aharon Jacob, a neighbor’s toddler, walked by with his mother following him.

“Hi, Mrs. Jacob,” she said. Mrs. Jacob had once been Leah’s Chumash teacher. She also taught the class the Haggadah before the holiday of Pesach.

Aharon looked up and smiled. He babbled incomprehensibly. Leah did not recognize any of the words. “Do you know what he is saying?” she asked Mrs. Jacob.

Her neighbor smiled. “When we don’t know what he is saying, and he sounds like he does, we usually answer him back in kind. I don’t like baby talk so I usually say, D’Tsach, Adash, B’Achav, the passuk from the Haggadah that Rabbi Yehudah composed.”

Aharon stopped, sat down on the ground, and answered his mother. It almost sounded like “D’Tsach, Adash, B’Achav”!

Lieutenant McCarthy stood up. “What are they saying?” he asked.

“That’s a mnemonic,” said Leah slowly. “It helps us remember things we want to memorize. This one stands for the Hebrew names of the Ten Plagues in Egypt, Dam, Tsefardaya, Kinim, Arov, Dever, Shechin ....” She stopped in midsentence. She looked at the paper the lieutenant had given her and she began to smile.

"I know other mnemonics," she said. "Now I remember! We learned them in Earth Science so that we would better remember the seven continents. We used to say: Eat An Aspirin After A Night Snack. That sentence stands for 'Europe, Antarctica, Asia, Africa, Australia, North America, and South America.' And, to remember the oceans we used to say 'I Am A Person' — the Indian, the Arctic, the Atlantic, and the Pacific. I think a geography teacher would carry these mnemonics to teach his class."

Lieutenant McCarthy jumped up and let out a "Whoopee!" He almost hugged Leah but stopped himself quickly. Mrs. Lamdan stepped outside. She looked at Leah and the lieutenant, at Mrs. Jacob and Aharon.

"Miracle of miracles," she said, "my headache has gone away. That karpas salad really worked!"

FINDERS KEEPERS

A TAANIS ESTHER MYSTERY

"School on a fast day just slows us down," said Leah Lamdan to her friend Rachel as they stepped out of the Bais Malkah High School building at noontime. A sigh escaped her lips, the sort of sigh that follows the kind of statement she had made. "On a day like today, the fast day before Purim, I smell the aroma of all the baked goodies for tomorrow. It wafts through my nose and mind and makes the fast more difficult.

"C'mon," laughed Leah. "It isn't that bad. The fast began early this morning and it's only lunchtime now."

"Do you hear my stomach growling?" Rachel asked jokingly. "I should be in bed or just taking it easy before I develop a headache." Suddenly she stopped speaking as she swiveled around to watch three police cars, with their sirens blaring, racing down the street. They stopped a block away from the school.

"What hap ...." she started to say, turning to Leah, who was also gawking at this same sudden intrusion. The girls crossed the street and moved forward with many of the students who were just exiting their classes.

The police created quite a stir. One officer jumped out of his car and ran into one of the houses on the block. Other officers immediately began stopping the flow of traffic while another began diverting the people heading in that direction.

"I don't hear an ambulance," Rachel shouted above the din. "Did someone get hurt?" She sounded afraid. She grabbed her friend by her sleeve and then made a ludicrous pun that Leah laughed at even through her irrational fear. "Are the police fast enough on this fast day?"

Leah cocked her eyebrow quizzically, hesitated, and stared at another car that seemed to be heading their way. She drew a deep breath as the car stopped in front of her, and Lieutenant McCarthy stepped out. He looked grim.

"Your father told me that you were probably leaving school about now," he remarked. "Today, he said, is a half-day of school and you're fasting."

"What is going on?" she asked.

"Mr. Kimoto was robbed in broad daylight, with his friends sitting there next to him."

Leah blinked. She shook her head. "Who is Mr. Kimoto?"

"A very rich man," he ventured. "He is one of the richest guys in this neighborhood. He lives in that house," he said, pointing toward the area where the policemen were milling around. "He lives here in this neighborhood because he doesn't want anyone to know how rich he is. He plays down his wealth. We know about him because he hired two private guards, former officers from our precinct, at very good pay, to protect him. As luck would have it, one of the guards is on vacation now and the other woke up sick this morning. I think Mr. Kimoto figured that for a day or two he could get along without protection."

"Why did you call my father?" Leah ventured to ask.

"When we got the call about the robbery, something bothered me. I couldn't figure out what it was, and I still can't. It was not your everyday kind of burglary, when the thief sneaks into the house late at night and steals things. This guy or gal did it while they were all sitting there. The thief has to be one of Mr. Kimoto's guests."

"What do you mean?" she asked evenly.

She gave him time to think it over. He fidgeted where he was standing and looked uneasy. "Your father said that it would be okay for you to come into the house with us as long as some windows are open. He says that you are fasting and you need fresh air."

Leah smiled as one of Rachel's elbows poked her in the ribs.

"Can I come, too?" she asked the lieutenant.

"Sorry," he said. "This is a crime scene. We can't have outsiders come in and mess up the crime scene."

"Oh, well, then, I'll wait for you out here for a while," Rachel said.

The lieutenant gestured toward the house. "I consider this a favor." He smiled faintly. "I'll explain what happened as we go inside," he said. "I don't want anyone leaving this house until we catch the thief."

She entered the house behind him in a pleasant frame of mind.

"This robbery took place perhaps an hour ago. Mr. Kimoto had invited a couple of friends to his house to view a ruby he wanted to sell. He planned on giving them the options first to bid on it and then to buy it. I'll tell you that he has an 'interesting' group of friends. One of his friends is Tony Luciano, a reputed mobster and jewel collector. The only reason he is not a wanted man is because we have no proof of his shenanigans. And then of course, there are his scare tactics. People are afraid to accuse him of any wrongdoing. Another guest is Madame Renée from the House of Voire in Paris. She is a well-known collector of interesting jewels. You may think that she is an innocent bystander, but rumors are that she is not allowed to return to Paris. And then there is Yedid Caspi from Israel, who owns an unusual collection of jewelry, so he says. Everyone knows he drinks too much and then has a tendency to speak 'with malice aforethought.'

"Of course, Mr. Kimoto greeted his guests and told them of his plans to sell the ruby. Yesterday, it seems, at different times during the day, they came over to study the jewel with loupes, those special lenses jewelers use, and today they expected to bid on it. They had agreed to this method before they showed up this morning."

"What happened?"

McCarthy frowned. "Mr. Kimoto removed the special box with the ruby in it from his safe and brought it out to show them again. While they waited for him to re-enter his office, they all agreed that it suddenly turned very hot in the room where they were sitting and waiting. All the lights had been turned on to make the room bright enough to view the stone properly. As he came back, he felt the heat and suggested that he would turn on the air conditioner. He put the open jewelry box on his desk and went over to turn it on. Suddenly the lights went out! It took several minutes to reach the circuit breakers and turn the lights on again. By that time, the jewelry box was empty and the ruby was gone! Mr. Kimoto was quite distraught and he insisted that no one leave the premises.

"He called the station and demanded that some officers come over immediately. He is a prominent citizen and the captain insisted that at least two cars go over to his house. I'm in charge and it frustrates me because this is going to be one of those cases that will be difficult to solve." It was a troublesome thought and he shifted his weight uneasily as he spoke.

"I take it that you've already searched his guests," said Leah.

"Mr. Kimoto insisted that we search him first so that no one could harbor any ill will against him. There have been some rumors, you see, that his business has not been going well. He claims that they are just rumors and all business men have their ups and downs. Anyway, he was clean as a whistle."

"And I assume that his guests were also clean," said Leah with a nod.

"Yep. Shall we meet the suspects? I consider them all suspects because if they are not suspected on this case, then they are on other cases."

Leah nodded and followed him into the den. She was surprised to realize that it was not as cold outside as it was in this house. Leah felt it was cold enough to leave out the milk! The window shades were down and darkened the room. The room looked as lively as a funeral parlor except it had austere portraits of people who were probably deceased. The faces in the frames stared down at her with terribly judgmental expressions.

The lieutenant introduced Leah to the people who were sitting and waiting. Leah asked, "Did anyone hear anyone move around when the room was dark? Could somebody have come in when the room was dark?"

"No," answered the lieutenant, "when the room unexpectedly went dark, Mr. Kimoto called one of the servants to come immediately with flashlights so they could see. Everyone remained seated in the library until she came in with a lit candelabra and walked with Mr. Kimoto to the circuit breaker on the wall. Once the light was back on, they all saw that the ruby was missing."

Leah frowned. "Was the ruby insured?" she asked.

"Of course," nodded Mr. Kimoto. "You would not expect that I would have it here in my house and not have it insured? But, really, I want to find it, not lose it." Mr. Kimoto had a glum expression on his face.

It was a subdued group waiting for an answer.

The lieutenant frowned again and cleared his throat. "I will use another room to interview each of you separately," he said. "My aide," he pointed to Leah," will take notes."

They all began to complain.

"I have no time for this."

"I must get back to my studio."

"I have a plane ticket to leave the country tonight after the reading of the Megillah."

Each of the guests wanted to be interviewed first and then be permitted to leave. Mr. Kimoto was even more upset.

"One of my guests is a thief," he countered. "I must know who dared to treat me in such a despicable manner."

"Listen, here," said Yedid Caspi. His face was red with anger. "Get a warrant if you want to keep me here. I am not staying of my own free will."

"You were always unsavory," replied Mr. Kimoto. "A leopard never changes its spots."

Mr. Caspi shook his fist and looked ready for a fight. "This is not the first time I heard you talk that way about me. I was once, a long time ago, mixed up with some no-good hoodlums, and this guy keeps making crazy accusations as if I am still involved with them. After I was released from prison, I got a decent job in a restaurant where Kimoto was a waiter. We both set higher goals for ourselves and we both succeeded. Leave me alone, Kimoto, and stop spreading your stories."

The lieutenant shook his head. He turned to Yedid Caspi. "Did you stay put when the lights went out or did you move around a little?"

He shrugged. "I'm not one of those people who take things easy. Something happens and I get up. There's nothing illegal about that! I was searched already and there is no reason for me to stay here."

"You will please remain until I speak to each of you," the lieutenant answered calmly. "I would like to finish up as soon as possible, just like you."

Madame Renée removed a cigarette from a diamond-studded case she was holding. The lieutenant leaned over with his lighter and lit the cigarette. She puffed, once, twice and drew a deep breath.

"May I?" asked the lieutenant, pointing to the cigarette case. She handed it to him and he opened it and moved some cigarettes around.

"The ruby could probably fit in here," he said.

"But it did not," she replied. "I don't need to steal to make my money. I am an expert in my field. And you know, walking around in this community today made me think of New Orleans."

"She means Purim," said Yedid Caspi to Leah. He smiled at the lieutenant's aide and saluted her. "I've heard of you," he continued. "Isn't it a fast day today? Tomorrow is Purim. Why are you here? Did you do all your baking and cooking for the seudah already?"

Leah felt uncomfortable but she did not answer. She stared at him with a hint of fear in her eyes.

Tony Luciano stood up. He shrugged his shoulders and nodded his head as he looked around the room. "When I do somethin', I know what I'm doin'. I have nothin' to do with this robbery. You can't keep me here and I won't stay. I let you search me ... somethin' I usually don't allow. That's enough of my time. I'm goin'."

"Please," said Leah. "May I look at the box that held the ruby?"

McCarthy turned to one of the officers, who nodded his head. The box had been dusted for prints already. Leah turned the box over in her hands and opened it, peering intently inside. Then she returned the box to Mr. Kimoto.

Leah then turned to the lieutenant. "Lieutenant," she whispered as he leaned down to hear her question.

"Mr. Kimoto," he said as he straightened up, "the box, please."

He placed the box into a white envelope and handed it to an officer with a note. There was grumbling around the room when the officer left the room but they all sat down again.

The lieutenant was reviewing his notes so he asked that the lights be turned up a bit. Leah sat there, quietly thinking, when the little lightbulb in her head lit up. That's what her brother Aharon called her sudden spurts of insight — a lightbulb aglow. Soon, the room was getting hot again. Leah stood up and went over to the air conditioner.

"Was it fixed?" she asked Mr. Kimoto. "Would you mind turning it on?"

Mr. Kimoto did not look happy. He pulled at his shirt collar and stretched it away from his neck. "Perhaps we should go into a different room. We are all tired and this delay is ridiculous."

The lieutenant turned on the air conditioner and the lights went out immediately.

"I guess the fuse box is not the problem," said Leah. "I think you wanted the lights to go out."

"Why?" came a chorus from everyone in the room. The lieutenant continued his questions.

"Why would he do that? And if so, did he take the ruby? Where is it?"

The officer returned just then and handed a note to the lieutenant. He studied it a minute and wrinkled his nose at Leah. He handed her the note and she smiled.

"Well, Mr. Kimoto," she said. "you're not Jewish and you do not have to fast today." Then she turned back to the lieutenant and smiled. "Mr. Kimoto must have reminded himself of the old days when he worked in a restaurant. He probably decided that the best way to hide the ruby would be by eating it. But he did not want to lose his precious stone. So he made sure the circuit would break when the air conditioner went on, turning the lights out. In the dark he ate his substitute ruby — that is, the cherry-red candy that was sitting in the box. I think he just wanted to collect the insurance on the ruby and put the blame on its loss on someone else. The lab found traces of melted sugar in the lining of the box."

Lieutenant McCarthy began to laugh. "Have an easy fast," he said to Leah, "and celebrate a very happy Purim."

The Room Number

A Purim Mystery

"It's me," Leah Lamdan called out as she entered her house, "I'm home." She stepped into the kitchen and looked around. Her shoulders slumped and she sighed as if some excitement had gone. A thought stirred in the back of her mind as she focused on the refrigerator. She smiled and enthusiastically opened the refrigerator door. She tapped her toe as she looked eagerly inside. On the top shelf toward the front of the refrigerator stood a bottle of ketchup, upside down. She stared dumbstruck for a moment and then laughed aloud in mock awe. "Moshe!" she said, referring to her creative younger brother. "Ours is the fastest ketchup in town. Now I know why!" Her smile widened as her she reached toward the back of the shelf and pulled out a brown lunch bag. Then she heard a key moving in the front door and the door opening.

"Leah, are you home?" Her mother's voice was brusque and her words came fast. "Leah? Is that you in the kitchen?"

"Ima, I'm home," Leah called out.

Mrs. Lamdan stepped briskly into the kitchen. She seemed somewhat impatient as she removed the jacket of her check suit and placed it on the back of a chair.

"I brought my schoolbooks home," Leah explained. "I thought I'd take a snack before going to Manhattan. Shaindy says that the Columbus Day specials include plenty of discounted clothes."

Mrs. Lamdan smiled admiringly at her daughter. "Just be careful. When I was your age, I don't think my parents had to worry if I traveled to Manhattan, but today, the world is very different." She waved her hand and added, "People are different, too."

"I know, I know," nodded Leah. "But my group of friends is going together. We're meeting at the subway at 12:30 and we hope to be in Macy's by 1:30. Then they'll come back together and I'll go to meet Sheryl."

"What time are you meeting Sheryl and her mother?"

"Three-thirty. I'm so excited to meet my pen pal at last. We've been corresponding for two years, and now, finally, we'll be meeting face to face," she confided with a little giggle.

Mrs. Lamdan grinned. "They came from Paris to spend only one day in Manhattan? It sounds unbelievable!"

"They're going to California tomorrow for a family wedding. They'll be there for at least two weeks." A thought recurred, which she expressed now to her mother. "Maybe on the way back …."

"We'll invite them here for a 'Brooklyn Day,'" Mrs. Lamdan finished Leah's thought and agreed. Leah was delighted. She threw her mother a kiss and waved goodbye as she ran out of the house toward the subway to meet her school friends. What an exciting day was planned!

◇◇◇

At 3:30 Leah was standing at the information desk at the Stern's Hotel in Manhattan. She was tired and unhappy. The noise and clamor of the big department store had made her feel shellshocked. Nothing in the store had been to her liking, she was tired, and she would have loved to be at home already with her shoes off.

"I'm supposed to meet Mrs. Munk and her daughter Sheryl," she told the desk clerk.

"Your name, please?" he said brusquely, as if too busy to deal with her. Then he scowled and turned aside. Leah summoned up a weak smile.

"Leah," she said. "My name is Leah Lamdan."

The clerk turned toward a mail slot and pulled out a folded note. "A message for you," he said coldly.

Leah unfolded the note and frowned as she read it. How much worse could the day get! Sheryl and her mother were delayed at the biggest department store in the world, Macy's. Could Leah wait until 4 o'clock? They would surely return by then!

Leah tried to quell the annoyance she felt at having to wait in the hotel when she had been at the same store where they were now shopping. She stood quietly next to the desk and glanced at the big clock behind the clerk.

"Is there a place I can wait for them?" Leah asked him.

"We have a big lobby," he replied. "Maybe you know some of our guests and could be invited to wait in their room."

Leah shook her head. "The only guests I know are the Munks."

"Well, floors six to fifteen are college dormitory floors. Maybe you know one of the students?"

"I doubt it," said Leah. "I didn't even know that the hotel houses a dormitory."

"Well, for your information, floors one through five are for regular paying guests."

"The Munks probably have a room on one of those floors," she said earnestly.

"I'm not at liberty to say," he said. "We have an even 100 rooms on every floor. The first digit of the room number is the floor number and after that is the room number. If you know how to count, you can't get lost in our hotel." The middle-aged clerk stroked his neatly trimmed beard and smiled at his own witticism.

Leah smiled back. "Thanks, but that doesn't help me. I guess I'll just wait here for my friends." She looked around the lobby. It was a nice lobby, not too big and not too small. Chairs and sofas placed in strategic locations served to divide the room into separate areas, creating cozy conversation areas. A newsstand filled the far end near the elevators, next to a bank of public telephones. A small sign was fastened to the wall near the elevator doors. Leah walked over to study the sign. The word "College" was printed in large letters at the top, and the phrase "Floors 6 to 15" was added below. A man standing next to the newspaper stand looked impatiently at his watch and then stared back at the elevator doors.

"Are you going up, too?" he asked Leah.

Leah shook her head, "No."

"The dormitory is on floors six to fifteen. Aren't you a student here?"

"No," she said. "I'm not a student here," she said, walking away from him toward the telephone booths. She sighed and looked at her watch. She had arranged to meet her Uncle Aharon at 5 o'clock at the 47th Street subway. Should she call him now and tell him she might be delayed, or should she wait until later? She looked around the hotel lobby again, walked over to a comfortable leather couch, and sat down to wait.

Half-an-hour, she thought. *What can I do for half-an-hour?* She pulled out her pocket Tehillim and opened it to the psalms recited on the second day of the week. Quietly she began to read some of the psalms to herself. *There is something special about saying Tehillim when you are alone,* she mused. *It's quite comforting.*

"Excuse me," apologized a tall, thin, well-dressed red-haired young woman. She cleared her throat as she glanced at Leah, hesitating a moment, but then she looked anxious to talk.

"I'm sorry to bother you," she repeated as she leaned over. "Are you Jewish?"

Leah looked at her curiously and then noticed that the young woman was pointing to the Tehillim that Leah was holding.

"I'm Jewish too!" the woman said as she quickly glanced around the room. She sat down next to Leah. "My name is Eleanor, Eleanor Levitansky. Are you staying in this hotel?" At first glance Eleanor seemed poised and professional. Leah was surprised that she had approached a total stranger. A warning bell rang inside her head.

"I'm Jewish too," repeated Eleanor Levitansky. "My brother had a Bar Mitzvah a long time ago and I remember practicing the blessing for the Torah with him. I learned the Hebrew alphabet when I was younger. That's how I recognized that the book you are holding is in Hebrew. But I really don't remember the names of the different letters anymore. Is it a prayer book?"

Leah kissed her Tehillim and closed it. "It's a Tehillim, the *Psalms*," she said as she looked toward another chair. *Should I change my seat?* she thought nervously.

"Are you a guest of the hotel or are you a student?" Eleanor asked.

"Neither," said Leah quietly. "I'm waiting for someone."

"Oh!" Eleanor sighed sadly. "I wish you had a room here. I'd be willing to pay you to let me sleep here tonight!"

"I don't understand," said Leah. "Is the hotel full?"

"Most of the hotels are packed this Columbus Day weekend. Lots of people like to come to New York for the parade, the sales, the long vacation weekend. There are lots of conventions this weekend, also. It's difficult to get a room."

Leah shook her head. "I'm sorry," she said, and meant it. "I wish I could help you but I don't live in Manhattan."

"I understand," said the young woman. "I'm here only for the night. I have an important interview tomorrow morning with a company I've been waiting to join. A friend of mine was married yesterday. She and her husband planned on spending their first week as a married couple in New York City. They reserved a suite here, but at the wedding, a relative surprised them with tickets for two to Israel. So now they are at the airport ready to fly off to the Holy Land."

"And their room here ...?"

"They called the hotel to cancel their reservations. The manager told them that they are responsible to pay for one day of their stay, and he was charging their credit card. They knew that I had plans to come to New York, so they offered me the room for the one night. It's paid for anyway."

"You mean that you will be alone in a whole suite?" Leah said amiably.

Eleanor grimaced and massaged her lower back. "I am nowhere." She pulled out a thin piece of plastic about the size of a credit card. "This is the room key. You slide it into a slot in the door of your room and then turn the knob. If the card is put into the wrong door, or inserted the wrong way, then the door will not open."

"So you *do* have a room!" Leah said gleefully. "What a lucky person you are, to be given a free room."

"But," Eleanor looked annoyed, "the key card doesn't have a room number printed on it. The room combination is impressed on it magnetically, and it is wiped clean at check-out time."

Leah felt impatient. "So how do you know your room number?" she asked.

Eleanor looked hurt. "That's the problem! The hotel sent my friend a different card with the room number on it," she explained.

"Good," said Leah. "So now you know that you have a room and the key card to enter it."

"But I don't know the room number! My girl friend kept it by mistake. The newlyweds were in a rush to leave for the airport. After all, the tickets were a surprise gift! My friend showed me the card and said, 'This is the room number. Don't turn it upside down!" Then she handed me the key card and rushed out to the taxi with her husband. She forgot to give me the card with the room number."

Leah leaned back on the couch. "Wow! What a dilemma! Why don't you call her?"

"I told you — they're on their way to Israel right now!" Eleanor could not conceal her exasperation.

"How terrible!" Leah sympathized. "Why don't you ask the manager at the desk? Tell him your girlfriend's name and he'll tell you the room number."

"I don't remember her married name. I only met her fiancé once before the wedding, and I didn't bring the invitation to New York with me."

Leah observed her carefully. "Maybe the manager will let you look at the register and you will recall the name."

"I asked him already. He is not allowed to show me the list of registered guests. He says that he is not even permitted to tell me if a guest is registered. It's called 'invasion of privacy.'"

Suddenly Leah remembered that the clerk had refused to tell her if the Munks were registered. She realized that Eleanor was telling the truth.

Eleanor looked at Leah in despair. "I thought maybe I could use the key card on all the rooms, but I'm afraid I'll be arrested for attempted burglary!" She sighed bitterly. "Heh! I need my rest tonight! I came to New York City with a great presentation. I know that my new bosses will like it. I must do well at the meeting tomorrow! I need a good night's sleep. At 9 o'clock tomorrow morning I must be relaxed and confident. Now, please tell me, how can I be?" She looked exasperated.

"What do I do now? I won't be able to sleep tonight. There are no rooms available in a decent hotel. I must stay in Manhattan because of my early interview. I have no time or patience to travel. There's a room in this hotel for me and I don't know which!" Suddenly she stopped talking and stood. She stared down at Leah and said sarcastically, "Do you think your psalms could help?"

Leah fingered her place in the Tehillim carefully. "One of my mother's good friends became ill suddenly. The doctors told the family that she had a one percent chance of survival. People in the yeshivahs and girls' schools heard about her case and launced a Tehillim campaign in her merit. All over, here and in Israel, Tehillim was said for her, for Chava Yehudis bas Rivkah. Two days later, Baruch Hashem, the doctors called her a 'miracle woman.' She was alert and responsive. She is miraculously alive today!"

"Well, even if they prayed for your mother's friend, I'd guess that they really wouldn't be interested in my promotion." Eleanor brushed it off. "But if your Tehillim can help me now, I promise that I will try to learn more about being Jewish and I will try to say a psalm every day. By the way, how many psalms are there?"

Leah looked at her Tehillim. "There are 150 chapters," she said quietly. "The psalms were written by King David and they are the expression of our thoughts and emotions before Hashem. They express our trust in Hashem." She opened her Tehillim again, turned to Psalm 46, and quietly began to translate the Hebrew into English for Eleanor. Suddenly she stopped and stared at Eleanor. "Hashem can turn man's plans upside down," she said. "I think I know the answer to your dilemma. How would you like to try your key card in the doors of only two rooms?"

"What do you mean — two rooms? There are 100 rooms in this hotel!" Eleanor gawked. She was beginning to think that Leah was delusional.

"Just two rooms. I think one of them may be yours and if I am wrong, you'll be no worse off than you are now."

Leah placed her finger on her lip in the typical gesture she used when she believed she had solved a problem, smiled, and nodded her head. Eleanor Levitansky stared back at Leah and then shrugged her shoulders.

"If you're right, I will stick by what I said about learning more about Judaism. Tell me which rooms — I'll try anything!"

They were very lucky. The first room was the right one. Eleanor hugged Leah and walked her back to the lobby. Just then, Sheryl and her mother returned from Macy's. When they heard Eleanor's story, they were very impressed.

"How did you know?" they asked Leah.

Leah smiled and held her Tehillim tightly. "Well, Eleanor told me that when her friend showed her the room number, she advised Eleanor not to turn the plastic card upside down. I guess that she did not want to mislead her. As we know, the top ten floors are dorm rooms, so the room could only be on floors one to five. The first digit of the room number could be one, two, three, four, or five. The numerals two, three, four, or five don't read as numbers if they are upside down. So only number one remains as a number you can read either way. The last digit of the room number could be any number from zero to nine, but anything over five is eliminated, since if the card would be turned upside down, the last digit would become the first, which again can only be from one to five. The last digit must also be 'one,' as it is still the only number that could be turned upside down and be read as a number. Now we know that the room number is one-something-one. That *something* is the middle digit. Again, we consider the digits from one to nine. Zero, one, six, eight, and nine can also be looked at upside down as zero, one, nine, eight, and six. The room numbers 101, 111, or 181 look the same upside down as right side up. That leaves 161 or 191 as numbers that change when turned over. So we tried 161 first and we were lucky right away. The key card opened the door."

Leah then opened her Tehillim to Psalm 46. "Our Rabbis explain that in this psalm, King David foresaw the Babylonian and Persian exiles. When David fled from his son Avshalom, Shimi ben Gera of the tribe of Binyamin cursed David. Yet David did not allow his men to kill Shimi because he foresaw that Mordechai the Jew was destined to come from Shimi's family. For this reason, the great tzaddik, the Vilna Gaon, recited this psalm on Purim, the holiday when we say, '*V'nahapoch hu!*' We believe that Hashem turns things upside down to help His people.

"Eleanor approached me while I was reading this psalm. She mentioned the upside-down card and I thought of this psalm, this psalm for Purim and the *V'nahapoch hu*. Room 161 was the correct room."

Eleanor Levitansky stared in amazement. "Tonight I'll be able to sleep," she said. "And tomorrow I'll make my presentation. But win or lose, after that, I will say a psalm of praise to Hashem!"

THE RANSOM

A PESACH MYSTERY

Leah Lamdan opened the door and stepped inside. "Anyone home?" she called out casually as she slammed the door shut behind her. It was Chol Hamoed Pesach and she had left the house early in the morning, riding the Bikur Cholim bus to visit people in the hospital. Now she was home and she did not know what to expect. She suddenly remembered that her mother had mentioned that on Chol Hamoed she planned to visit a friend who was finally, Baruch Hashem, home from the hospital, "Oh well," Leah said, half to herself. "It's Pesach. Let's see what's in the fridge."

She thought she heard footsteps behind her and quickly turned to see her father coming into the kitchen and smiling at her. "Today I must go to the Golds and thank them for their pre-Pesach donation. Their gift to our *Matanas*

L'Evyonim campaign this year really helped many of the Kollel people in the yeshivah. What a mitzvah!"

Leah looked surprised. "You're thanking them for performing a mitzvah?"

"I'm thanking them because they included *me* in their mitzvah. They insisted that both of our families share the mitzvah. Based on my income and what I felt that I could give, he gave 200 times that amount! Mr. Gold told me that he feels that since I was the one who encouraged him to donate the first time he participated in the campaign, my yearly encouragement has helped his company become very profitable. He claims that he has made our yeshivah a 'secret partner' in his company and, as his profit increases, he gives more *matanos* to the rebbeim."

Leah smiled. "I guess Mr. Gold sees you as a good adviser."

"That sounds like a good profession. 'Adviser for profits.' I only hope that I continue to be so wise," he replied. "Now, what brings you home so early?"

"I went on the Bikur Cholim bus this morning," she answered. "It's hard to believe the number of people who need help daily! Hospitals and nurses are swamped with work, and whatever we can do to make it easier for the patients is really a mitzvah. What did disturb me, though, is the number of police officers out there searching for someone or something. Did you hear about any new terrorist warnings?"

Rabbi Lamdan shook his head. "Not terrorists. I did hear that there is a gang of thieves — actually, kidnappers — preying on families."

"Kidnappers! I remember reading that they do that in order to get a ransom. They kidnap someone and threaten to harm him unless a big ransom is paid."

Rabbi Lamdan frowned. "Where did you read about such things?"

"When we were reviewing Parshas VaYishlach and the kidnapping of Dinah, one of the girls in class asked about other famous captives. Morah Zimmerman told us the story of Reb Meir of Rothenberg, you know, the Maharam D'Rottenberg. He was held captive for seven years by Emperor Rudolph I of the Holy Roman Empire. The emperor demanded that the Jewish community pay an extremely large tax — 30,000 thousand marks — for his release. Although the amount was raised, the Maharam told his people not to pay the exorbitant price for fear that it would encourage the government to imprison other community leaders. The Maharam died in prison in 1293. Finally, 14 years after his passing, Reb Alexander ben Shlomo Wimpen paid a lesser price, but still most of his personal wealth, so that the body would be returned to the community for proper burial. Reb Alexander requested that his body would be buried next to the Maharam's kever."

Rabbi Lamdan confirmed Leah's remarks. "When the Maharam was in prison, many halachic questions were asked of him and his answers were recorded by Rav Shimshon ben Tzaddok."

Leah smiled and nodded. "This story sounds like a future report for school," she laughed.

Her father checked his watch and continued, "Perhaps one of the most famous captives in our century was the Lubavitcher Rebbe, Rav Yosef Yitzchok, *zecher tzaddik livrachah*. He was thrown into the notorious Lubyanka prison in Russia on false charges. Public pressure helped free him in 1927 or 1928.

"Captivity has always terrified Jews because there are many laws that must be studied and practiced, and we are afraid that a captive may lose his Jewish identity. In fact, the government of Israel has a policy to do its utmost to free any soldiers captured by the enemy. A few years ago, more than 1,000 Arab prisoners were freed in exchange for one Jew. Every soldier in Israel knows that the government will try to free him if he is captured."

Leah found this information quite interesting. "Does the Torah tell us a prescribed amount of ransom to pay for a captive?" she wanted to know.

Her father lapsed into silence and took a container of milk from the refrigerator. He poured some of the milk into a cup. Then he nodded to Leah and continued, "Halachically, there *are* prescribed amounts. We have a mitzvah called *pidyon shevuyim*. A Jew is required to donate money to help free a fellow Jew taken captive. However, if a man wants to pay more from his own pocket, he may. In fact a husband could pay up to ten times the value of his wife!" He grinned as he said the last sentence. "My family is worth so much to me! I don't know what I would do, chas v'shalom, in such a circumstance."

Leah sat beside him at the table after taking some Pesach cookies from a canister on the countertop. "I don't think that we are considered rich enough to worry about being kidnapped, but what about someone like Mr. Gold?"

Rabbi Lamdan sighed. "Success has made Mr. Gold even more thankful to Hashem. He is our yeshivah's longstanding philanthropist and we are thankful for whatever he gives. Let's hope that Hashem continues to keep him from harm. Are you working on some kidnapping case?"

"Oh no!" she laughed. "I don't think I know anyone rich enough to be kidnapped."

Rabbi Lamdan couldn't imagine anyone either. His looked relieved. Then, determined to remain in a good mood, he stood up and saluted Leah. "I am off to see Mr. Gold and share in a mitzvah we always do together. First we learn and then we recite our berachos."

Leah had finished her snack and had cleaned up the kitchen when the phone rang. She picked it up on the first ring. It was Mrs. Ackerman, who lived on the next block. Mrs. Ackerman began speaking rapidly, without the usual initial pleasantries. She sounded quite excited and clearly thought that she was speaking to Leah's mother as she called Mrs. Lamdan's name.

"Sarah," she began, "I must take Shimi to the doctor. He is running a high fever. Can you baby-sit for me right now? I can't leave Tully alone, and Dovid will soon come home from school."

Although she realized that Mrs. Ackerman had mistaken her for her mother, Leah did not bother correcting her. She knew that it was an emergency and answered, "I'll be right over."

As she hung up the phone she smiled to herself. The Ackermans' so far had only sons, seven of them! Mrs. Akerman's sister, Mrs. Mermelstein, who lived three doors away, had only daughters. Leah used to baby-sit for both families when the children were quite young, but as they grew older, she became exclusively the Mermelstein baby sitter. Now she was temporarily going back to the Ackermans.

Leah said the berachah acharonah for the cookies and milk (her mother's Pesach cookies were shehakol), put her jacket back on, and stepped outside again. It had suddenly turned very cold. The gusts of wind were so strong that as Leah walked down the street she thought to herself, *This is a setting for a mystery or some strange event.* She shivered and walked slowly to the Ackermans, who lived a block away.

When she stepped outside, she noticed that her father had not taken his car to the Golds. The Golds lived four avenue blocks away, and some avenues were almost triple the length of street blocks. Her mother would be happy to know that her father had begun exercising again by walking to his chavrusah's home.

Leah stopped in front of the Ackerman house. Even from the outside, it looked run-down. She shrugged her shoulders and rang the doorbell. Mrs. Ackerman was out the door in seconds and Leah turned her attention to Tully, who was an imaginative live wire. Leah knew that her ears and eyes had to be open and ready for Tully's antics.

Soon Dovid came rushing in. "Where's my mother?" he growled when he saw Leah seated on the floor next to Tully, who was playing with a toy.

"Your mother had to take Shimi to the doctor," explained Leah.

Dovid looked angry. He looked at Tully and then back at Leah. "I'm going to my friend's house," he said. "My mother knows that I like to go to play with Nissan Gold after school. We are good friends and today he disappeared."

Leah stood up immediately. She tried to control her expression so that the children wouldn't see that she was upset. "What are you talking about?" she asked

"One of my classmates told me that a big black car was standing in front of the school just when Nissan arrived. The driver of the car got out and told Nissan something that upset him. and then Nissan got into the car with the stranger and was driven away."

Leah shook her head slowly. "So, maybe there was an emergency at home. Why do you suspect something else?"

"Because," he said angrily, "Nissan would have left a message for me. And he didn't." He shook his head sadly. "Something has happened to my best friend."

Leah stared at him and frowned. "Maybe he couldn't find you and he told someone else to let you know that he had to leave and the other kid forgot to tell you," she reasoned.

"No!" he answered angrily. "That's not the way good friends are. Nissan would have looked for me to let me know. He would have told the stranger that he couldn't leave without telling me. We do almost everything together. We are so close that my mother says that we can read each other's mind." He stuck out his bottom lip and glared at Leah.

Leah almost smiled at his angry expression, but stopped herself because of the serious nature of their discussion. "If you can read each other's mind, why don't you know where he is?"

David frowned. He was troubled. The pangs of guilt he felt showed in his expression. He looked very serious. "I am afraid," he said hoarsely. "I am afraid that something has happened to Nissan."

Leah saw the fear in his eyes. She was surprised that he could express himself so well. She waved her hand in the air like a musician waving his wand. "Maybe he just had to go somewhere and he didn't have a chance to tell you," she said in an attempt to calm him.

"Not tonight!" he answered gruffly. "Tonight is our Chofetz Chaim night. Nobody would go away!"

Leah stared back at him. "What's a 'Chofetz Chaim night'?" she wondered aloud. She sat down on a stool next to the window to hear what Dovid had to say.

"Our Rebbi taught us the importance of not speaking *lashon hara*. Some of us in the class decided to read together from the Chofetz Chaim's sefer, *Guard Your Tongue*, once a week in order to learn the laws of *lashon hara*. We already made up a group of 55 boys from the yeshivah. Every Tuesday we meet in one of our homes to review our accomplishments, to be sure that we did not speak *lashon hara*, and to learn some more from the sefer. Nissan Gold would not go away and forget our meeting tonight." He bit his lip and rubbed his eye.

Leah half-turned on the stool and looked around the room. The window was open and she could smell the plants in the garden as the breeze blew through the room. Her friend Sarah Haber had tried to organize a similar Chofetz Chaim learning group in her neighborhood, but Leah had heard that no more than five classmates ever showed up. How had Nissan's group attracted so many participants?

Because of the wind, papers were strewn around the floor, so Leah decided to partially close the window. She then turned to Dovid again.

"Try calling him at home," she advised. "If he's not home then there is no sense in your going there."

Dovid stared back at her. He looked annoyed. "I already stopped at his house on my way home from yeshivah. Mr. Gold answered the door. He looked very unhappy. And he sounded strange!" Dovid furrowed his brow and scratched his head. He looked away from Leah and dropped his voice somewhat. "He looked strange," he repeated.

"Why do you say that? What did he say? How did he look?" asked Leah.

Pale and unwavering, Dovid gestured toward his own eyes to make a point. "Usually he is very friendly, but today he just stared at me and told me to go home. He said that Nissan had gone away!"

Leah sat down on the sofa and raised her eyebrows. *If his parents knew he had gone away, then he has not disappeared,* she thought. But Dovid had not finished speaking.

"I know that something has happened and Mr. Gold is trying to keep it from me. Nissan and I are like Dovid and Yonasan. We are closer than brothers. We feel each other's happiness and pain."

"Maybe," she tried to rationalize, "he will still show up tonight at your Chofetz Chaim night and then he will explain to you where he went so secretly and why."

"*Kain yehi ratzon*. So it should be," he replied soberly and quietly, "but I feel in my bones that something has happened to my friend. Will you help me?" His eyes turned pleadingly toward her.

She wore an amused expression. "Do your bones tell you where he may be?"

Dovid was serious. He turned silent for a few minutes. He shook his head. "He's not far from here," he answered.

Leah was at the door ready to leave. Mrs. Ackerman had told her that she could leave when Dovid showed up. Well, Dovid had arrived, so she could go home. But she hesitated at the door when she saw him so unhappy. His expression reminded her of a look her brother Aharon sometimes had when he felt burdened by some problem. It was a combination of reluctance and annoyance.

"When Mr. Gold opened the door, did you see my father?" she asked.

"He only opened the door a tiny bit," was the reply. "I couldn't see anything or anyone. But I thought I heard a lady crying. Does that make sense? Do you think Mrs. Gold was crying?"

Leah stared out the door and thought of the implications of what he was saying. She reminded herself of her previous conversation with her father and she was disturbed by that, too. Then she saw Mrs. Ackerman coming up the walk with Shimi in her arms. He looked half-asleep but he was whimpering softly. She looked back again at Dovid. He looked as if he were ready to cry.

"Thanks so much," said his mother. "Wait here a minute and I will pay you."

"Oh no!" said Leah. "This was a mitzvah call! There is no charge. That's what neighbors are for. We help each other out whenever necessary."

She then walked the three blocks to the Gold house. She felt uneasy about intruding at this time, but she rang the doorbell and waited.

Mr. Gold opened the door slightly. He was not happy. He looked as if he had been crying. "Leah Lamdan?" he asked hoarsely. He blinked at her as someone behind him murmured something. He looked back into the house for a moment and then opened the door wider. "Come in," he continued. "Your father is here."

She followed him through the large entrance hall into the beautiful dining room. Rabbi Lamdan was sitting at the table with an open gemara in front of him.

Mrs. Gold was also at the table, a box of tissues near her. She had obviously been crying.

"Well, well, well," began Mr. Gold. "Wonders of wonders! Nissim v'niflaos. Look who has come to join us. It is Leah Lamdan, herself." His voice was flat and tired. He pulled a handkerchief from his pocket and blew his nose. "How did you know to come? How did you know we want you?" he asked solemnly. "My son Nissan has been kidnapped!"

Leah stood awkwardly near her father. Rabbi Lamdan sat back in his chair and placed his fingertips together. "Mr. Gold got a phone call about 45 minutes ago from a voice he did not recognize. It was a man's voice. He was advised that Nissan had been kidnapped, as if we hadn't realized that already. Mr. Gold was told that no harm would come to his son if he would obey directions. He was warned not to contact the police. He must prepare $5,000 as ransom money for tomorrow."

Leah opened her eyes in surprise. "Five thousand dollars? That doesn't seem like much money for kidnappers to ask for," she said.

Rabbi Lamdan nodded. "I agree, but, in any case, the kidnappers said that they will call back tomorrow to tell him where to leave the money."

Leah frowned disapprovingly. "Did you call the police?"

"Of course not," said Mrs. Gold indignantly. "Do you think I want something even worse to happen to Nissan?"

"What makes you believe that the kidnappers won't harm him?" asked Leah. "Hasn't he seen them? Can't he identify them?"

Mrs. Gold paled. "How do you know ...?"

"Because Dovid Ackerman told me that some men in a car picked up Nissan in front of the yeshivah."

Mrs. Gold pressed her hand to her forehead. She did not look at Leah, but turned toward Rabbi Lamdan instead. "Do you think that she's right? Is it possible that we are doing more harm by not contacting the police?" She seemed afraid of his answer.

Rabbi Lamdan frowned. "It is possible that what Leah says is true. That's why I strongly urge you to contact the police."

Mr. Gold seemed to stare into space. "Nothing must happen to Nissan," he said. His eyes bored into Rabbi Lamdan and then he threw up his hands and muttered, "We'll call the police if you think that's best ...."

Mrs. Gold muffled a cry. A chill ran up Leah's spine. She swallowed hard and stared at her father. Rabbi Lamdan was scowling. He took a deep breath and then turned to his daughter.

"No!" he contradicted himself. "*They* can not contact the police. Who knows? The kidnappers may be watching the house and they'll see if the police arrive. *We* will do it! We'll go and explain everything to Lieutenant McCarthy."

Leah and her father did not speak during the short walk home and during the car ride to the police station. The lieutenant was busy with some paperwork when they walked in, but immediately put it aside to listened intently to Rabbi Lamdan's report.

He frowned and said, "The kidnappers informed the Golds immediately that Nissan had been snatched. They warned him not to contact the police. We know of this group. This is their M.O., their *modus operandi*," the Lieutenant said, using the Latin expression meaning, "the way they work." He stood, went to the office door, and called to another officer to join them.

Sergeant Reid nodded grimly to the Lamdans as he was introduced. Then he sat down and Rabbi Lamdan repeated the story again. Sergeant Reid spun his chair around to face Leah and her father. There was anger in his eyes and when he spoke his voice was stern.

"This is the sixth such case in New York City in the past six months. But this is the first time that we'll be in on it from the beginning, before any payment is made. In all the other cases, the parents paid the $5,000 and then they paid again and again. You see, the kidnappers ask for the first $5,000 to see how desperate the parents are. They don't return the kidnapped child. The next day they ask for another $5,000. And still they don't return the child. The kidnappers try one more time. Two families spent $15,000 before contacting the police; the other four spent twenty grand before they finally called us. When the kidnappers realize that the police have been contacted, they know that they will not receive more money and they release the child. He is usually found a few blocks from his home. So far, the child has not been not harmed or hurt in any way."

Leah pursed her lips. "This has happened before and no one in the community knew about it?" she said incredulously.

There was a prolonged silence. "Where did the other kidnappings take place?" Rabbi Lamban finally asked.

Sergeant Reid weighed his words. "Two in Queens, one in Riverdale, up in the Bronx, two from Staten Island, and one other in our precinct here in Brooklyn," he answered. "We shared information from the other precincts to learn more about their M.O."

Rabbi Lamdan raised a quizzical brow. "You have no clues regarding who they are and why they are doing this?"

Lieutenant McCarthy smiled grimly. "They are doing it for the ransom money."

"Since this is not the first time, were the police ever able to wait for the kidnappers and follow them?"

Sergeant Reid exchanged a brief look with the Lieutenant. "Yes," he acknowledged, "and we lost them." He scowled and consulted his notes. "There is more than one person involved in this plan. They are very organized. We guess that there are eight or ten young men involved."

"How is the money-drop carried out?" asked Leah.

"In all the previous cases, the father was ordered to deliver the money, packed into a paper grocery bag, to the designated place. He was met at a busy intersection where lots of people are around. Someone bumped into him, handed him a card, and took the paper bag full of money. The card states that the family will be contacted soon. Not a word is exchanged. After about two hours, one of the gang calls the house to say that they want more money. And they repeat the whole scenario. By the third and fourth times, the parents are very anxious and overwrought. The kidnappers probably think that the parents call in the police at this time. So the next call just informs the parents where the child can be found.

"They do this every time, but since there are so many people walking around at the drop-off point, we're not sure whom to grab. That's why we think that there may be eight or ten individuals involved, all walking back and forth among the innocent bystanders, just to confuse us. Last time, we made a mistake and grabbed the wrong man. He didn't have any money on him, and surely not a bagful! We don't even know for sure if that guy was part of the gang. These guys all walk around in different directions and we don't have the manpower to follow them."

Leah frowned and shook her head. She looked puzzled. "What makes you think that the kidnappers keep the child in a place not far from the home?"

"We have our own reason to believe that. But even if the child is hidden within two miles in each direction, that is a lot of space to cover. As I said before, this gang is very organized and synchronized. I don't think that the gang member who takes the money from the father is the one who holds it all the time. I think the paper bag is passed around like a football and when one suspects that an officer is nearby, he just passes it to someone else. Mr. Gold will probably be called tonight or early tomorrow morning to inform him where he should bring the money. They'll give him time to get to the bank and get the cash."

Leah pressed a hand to her mouth as if to hold in the words and the pain. "What will you do?" she asked.

"We must go to the Gold's house. We'll dress in plainclothes so that no one will suspect that we are the police. We will put a tracer on his telephone, although the conversation is usually so short that there's no time to trace the call. We will also check out different locations in the neighborhood. We must check every apartment that was rented in the past three or four months. You should check your synagogue bulletin board announcements or any community newspapers that advertise apartments for rent. The boy is being held in a rented apartment; that's part of the gang's M.O."

Sgt. Reid stood up and walked them to the door. He decided that he had to know more and that he had to catch these criminals. "Leah Lamdan," he began, "I heard about you from the lieutenant. I feel this seemingly random encounter of ours today in this police station will bolster our confidence and together we will defeat this gang. If you have any suggestions, I am ready to hear them. Please feel free to contact me anytime about this case."

"Do you think that you'll be able to find the apartment?" she asked

Sgt. Reid paused to think. He stepped out into the corridor, which had an air of age and mustiness even though the building was actually quite modern. Reid glanced quickly at his watch and then at Leah. He walked a few paces and then started back and stopped in front of her.

"You know what I think?" he asked rhetorically. "This was no random meeting here today. Your G-d wants you to solve this case as quickly as possible. I think that you're going to find that apartment and help us free that kid."

Leah stared at him silently, then left the police station with her father.

Later that evening, Dovid Ackerman came to Leah's house. "Nissan was not at our Chofetz Chaim learning group," he told her. "Did you check out what I told you?"

"I think I will need your help," she said. "If you want to help your friend Nissan, you must make sure not to speak *lashon hara*, especially tonight and tomorrow. Tell your friends that, too," she emphasized.

Dovid's glance darted all around the room. "I was right," he whispered hoarsely. "Something is wrong!" He left Leah's house impressed by his intuition and depressed by the thought that something bad had happened to Nissan. He did not ask Leah any more questions but ran to tell his chevrah the importance of keeping the laws of *shemiras halashon*.

The rest of the evening, Nissan's kidnapping filled Leah's thoughts, as did the details of *Parashas VaYishlach*, which discusses the kidnapping of Dinah, the daughter of Yaakov Avinu. She was kidnapped by Shechem because he wanted her to be his wife. Her brothers, Shimon and Levi, were furious that their sister could be stolen from them. Our Rabbis explain that Shechem knew that Yaakov's family members were successful entrepreneurs and he felt that his people could triple their income by being financially associated with the Hebrews. Shimon and Levi killed the people of Shechem and brought their sister home. Kidnappers were to be punished by death!

Leah also remembered that in the Middle Ages, Jews who had been kidnapped were sold as slaves. Pidyon shevuyim meant that the community bore the responsibility to buy the slaves their freedom, since ransoming captives is one of the 613 Commandments found in the Torah.

After supper, Leah's mind vacillated between her studies and Nissan's disappearance. What was one to do? How could they catch the kidnappers and free Nissan? She fingered the pen in her hand as she leaned back and closed her eyes. She thought about pidyon shevuyim and Nissan Gold. That was how the idea came to her.

Her father was not home, and her mother was busy in the kitchen. "Ima," she said softly. "I would like to go over to the Golds for a little while." Leah was not sure how much information her father had divulged to her mother, and was reluctant to tell her more.

"I know that something serious is happening," said Mrs. Lamdan. "Tizku l'mitzvos, may you merit to perform additional mitzvos."

Leah put on her light jacket and ran to the Gold's house. She was out of breath when she got there. Mr. Gold opened the door and led her into the kitchen.

"My wife is resting," he said. "This has taken a terrible toll on her health. I have already doubled my tzedakah donations for the year. Do you think that that will help?"

Leah nodded her head. "Our Rabbis say that giving charity saves lives. So of course your tzedakah will help. I was thinking about something else — something we can do that might help rescue Nissan."

Just then Lieutenant McCarthy and Sergeant Reid, dressed in civilian clothing, emerged from a room behind the kitchen. Leah told them her plan. Mr. Gold nodded his head, left the kitchen, and returned in minutes with an envelope of money. "Buy as many as you need," he told her. "I want my Nissan back!"

"There is something else I would like," said Leah.

The lieutenant nodded as he listened to her. "I like your plan," he said, "but the police department can't —"

"I'll pay for it all, "said Mr. Gold. "Just bring my Nissan home."

On the way home, Leah stopped at Dovid Ackerman's house. All his friends were there saying Tehillim.

"Good, I'm glad you're all here," she told the boys. "All of you can help me with my plan, but Dovid will synchronize and direct the arrangements."

◇◇◇

The next morning, the third day of Chol Hamoed Pesach, Mr. Gold received the call from the kidnappers. He was told how and where to deliver the money. After returning from the bank, Mr. Gold left the house in a better mood than he had experienced the previous day.

Lieutenant McCarthy warned him not to look so jubilant. "The kidnappers will suspect something," McCarthy told him. "Look worried and anxious."

Holding the bag of money tightly pressed against his side, Mr. Gold walked along the busy street. It seemed to him to be busier than usual, although he didn't usually walk casually through the neighborhood, spending most of his time at his office. He reasoned that it was Chol Hamoed and many people didn't go to work, so they had time to stroll about, shopping and passing the time with their friends and neighbors. The street was crowded with people ... and children. He even observed Nissan's friends riding their bikes on the avenue. Finally, someone with a wide-brimmed hat pulled low over his face tapped him on the shoulder and handed him a card. The man took the paper bag of money from Mr. Gold. Then he seemed to disappear. Where had he gone? Lots of people were moving around, and Mr. Gold was surprised by the suddenness of the turn of events. The hustle and bustle was still all around him; in fact, he was almost run over by a bike!

When he had returned home and showed the police the card, they confirmed that this conformed to the M.O. used by the kidnappers. But they were waiting to hear the message that they were hoping for.

By midday the call came in. McCarthy gleefully went to the Lamdans to share the good news. "Nissan is home," he said. "We have captured the gang. Your plan worked."

Leah closed her Tehillim and clapped her hands. She was excited, too "Baruch Hashem!" she repeated. "Baruch Hashem!"

Rabbi Lamdan beamed. "Okay, Leah, now you can tell us; what was your suggestion?"

Leah smiled. "This was a very clever gang. The plan was actually similar to a football game, in which the ball is passed from one player to the next. These criminals passed the bag of money from one to the other, so that it was much more difficult for the police to catch them with the loot. The police complained that they did not have enough officers to follow all the members of the gang — even if they could identify all of them in the crowd — and catch them, so I asked Mr. Gold for money to purchase walkie-talkies, which I gave out to each of Nissan's friends."

Leah laughed. "I remember once reading that a Rav asked a thief why he robbed. 'What do you mean?' asked the thief. 'That's what I do for a living!' The Rav told this story to his congregation and advised them to learn from the thief to be as conscientious in doing the mitzvos of Hashem. These boys are marvelous. They are the ones to thank. They prepared themselves for this task by davening all morning, reviewing some of the laws of *lashon hara* and saying the whole Sefer Tehillim. Then they went to the place where Mr. Gold had been told to meet the kidnaper. These kidnappers were on the lookout for policemen, not boys riding bikes and playing ball. The boys followed them, and they did not know it.

"Each boy chose one window-shopper who seemed to be just strolling around without a purpose. They called Dovid Ackerman on their walkie-talkies to tell him which person they were following, so that every boy had a different 'shopper.' Their task was just to follow their chosen window-shopper for about a half-hour. Each boy had his man, and followed him cautiously until the man went into a building. It turned out that most of the 'shoppers' went into the same building, even though they didn't seem to know each other. Some people went to other locations. The boys called in to the precinct to say where they were. The lieutenant figured that the building where most of the shoppers had gone was probably the hideout.

"A few minutes later, a big dirigible balloon flew above the building, advertising for one of the local stores. 'Look, look!' people shouted to one another. 'An airship!' They didn't know that it was *our* airship!" Leah smiled happily.

Sergeant Reid continued. "Those boys did a great job! We discovered that eight of the strollers or shoppers ended up in the same apartment building within a half-hour of the money being taken. So now we were pretty sure we knew which building Nissan was in, but we had to know — which apartment. The kidnappers were precise and cautious. How could we find Nissan in that apartment house?"

Lieutenant McCarthy took up the story. "Well, the first thing the men did was count the money. They were in for a big surprise! They had asked Mr. Gold for the usual $5,000, but the bag contained $7,000. They were shocked and they didn't know what to do. They contacted their leader, who had not met them at the building, and told him of their surprise. Mr. Gold had also paid for the dirigible which flew above the building.

Listening devices in that dirigible balloon picked up the phone call and then we knew the apartment number. We sent men into the apartment through the fire escape and through the doors at the same time, and caught the gang inside. We freed Nissan Gold and the men told us where to find their ringleader. A team of my officers is picking him up right now."

"What did it say on the tail of the dirigible?" asked Sergeant Reid. "It looked like a sentence or something ...."

"It was a quotation from Pirkei Avos, *Ethics of Our Fathers*. 'Rabbi Yehudah haNasi, the author of the Mishnah, used to say. "Consider three things and you will not sin. Know what is above you: A watchful eye, an attentive ear and all your deeds are recorded in a Book."'"

"Thank you, Leah," chuckled Sergeant Reid. "That statement is apropos. Enjoy the rest of your holiday. It was a pleasure working with you."

"Thank you, Leah," smiled Lieutenant McCarthy. "It's *always* a pleasure to work with you."

THE GREAT ADVENTURE

A CHOL HAMOED PESACH MYSTERY

"Oh, no!" Rachel Lehrgaff wailed. "What did I do?" Her bawl dissolved into a sob. Tears quivered on her cheeks. "Why did this have to happen to me now?" she sniffed as a tear dripped from the end of her nose onto the front of her blouse.

It was Chol Hamoed Pesach and the juniors of Bais Malkah High had decided to spend the day together in a theme park in New Jersey. The park had been rented out for the day by a tzedakah organization. The girls were excited to go together and a special bus had been chartered to take them there. One of the students assigned to collect signatures and money from the attendees was Rachel, and now, as she stepped off the bus, she slipped and fell.

Leah Lamdan was right behind her and she ran over to see how she could help. Rachel's liquid brown eyes met Leah's with an anguished look because of the pain and the embarrassment of "feeling like a klotz."

"I think," Leah began cautiously as girls got off the bus and encircled Rachel and Leah, "someone should call Hatzolah. I assume they are here."

"Oh, yes, I know they're here because I made the call to the organizers," Rachel answered. "But I don't know if I really need to bother them. Maybe if I rest a little, it will be all right. I need someone to help me get to that bench over there." She tried to lift herself from the ground. *"Ay yai yai yai!"*

She fell back as a Hatzolah volunteer came running over. The girls recognized Mr. Goldman, a teacher from a school a block from theirs. He shooed away all the other girls as he bent down to examine Rachel's ankle.

"I don't think it's broken," he said, "but it'll need an x-ray to tell for sure. It's swelling up already, so I'll have to stabilize the foot and pack it with ice to reduce the swelling."

He and Leah helped Rachel to the bench. "You must keep your foot elevated until someone comes to take you for the x-ray," he said. He went off to find ice at one of the kosher concessions that had opened for Chol Hamoed.

Rachel was crying again as she rubbed her eyelids. "My parents went away for the day. I can't reach them. I'll just sit here and wait until it's time to go home."

Leah looked around at all their friends, then turned back to Rachel. "We'll each take turns sitting with you for a half-hour, so you won't be alone. Right, girls?" she said. The friends agreed and they quickly arranged a schedule whereby two girls would spend time with Rachel for about a half-hour and then be relieved by another couple of friends.

Shifra Haber turned to Leah. "I'll be here the first hour," she said generously. "When all of you report on which rides you like best, I'll know which to go on first."

Leah smiled and looked at Shifra in undisguised admiration. "I'll join you for the first shift," she said.

Rachel laughed in pure disbelief mingled with relief that she wouldn't have to sit alone all day. "I don't want to take you away from the fun," she said. "I have my Tehillim with me and look — I can wiggle my toes already." Leah and Shifra insisted on staying with her until the next two girls returned.

Mr. Goldman returned with the ice and draped bags of it over Rachel's ankle. As he walked away, instructing Rachel to stay off her feet as much as possible, a big car pulled up near the entrance to the park. A young boy, about 3 or 4 years old, clambered out of the car, followed by his mother.

"Who's that?" asked wide-eyed Rachel, staring at the limousine with a half-smile on her lips.

The other two girls simply shrugged. Shifra blinked and yawned as she sat down on the bench. Leah removed a drink from her bag and with a quick grin offered it to her friends.

A police officer walked by. He stared at the girls and began talking into his walkie-talkie. He sucked in a deep breath as he raised his brows. He glared at the big car parked near the entrance and walked over to it. He bent down and spoke to the driver. The officer frowned, shook his head, and moved behind the car to guide it away from the entrance. The girls watched as the car moved forward and backward as the driver maneuvered it into a position that would allow him to drive away.

After the car had gone, the officer came back to the girls. "I see that you've hurt your ankle. Why don't you move to a more comfortable bench, inside to the right? If you're going to be sitting here, you may as well be comfortable. Down the block from that bench there's a store that carries all kinds of games and books," he said. "Maybe you can get one of those to help pass the time. If you need anything, ask for me. The name is Officer Daniel, and I'll be glad to help any way I can."

The girls thanked him for the information and for his concern. Just then an agitated woman approached him, pushing a cute three-year-old in a stroller. She looked around uncomfortably and tugged gently at her snood, making sure she was completely tzniusdik. "Someone took my wig," she told the officer. "I was wearing a wig when I got to the park, but when I go on a water ride, I change into a snood. I put my blond wig into a bag inside the bag of my stroller while I was on the ride with my toddler. I left the stroller in the waiting area, with all the other strollers. I can't believe that such a thing has happened to me! Someone took my wig!" she repeated in amazement.

"Maybe you put it into the wrong stroller," said Officer Daniel with a gentle smile. "Come into my office and fill out a report. We'll see what we can do." He then nodded to the girls and led the distraught woman to his office.

The girls began saying their daily Tehillim. Afterwards, Rachel tried calling home, but to no avail. Shifra went to the store to find a crossword-puzzle book. The theme of the first puzzle was about feet, she told the girls when she returned.

"Feet?"

"Yes," said Shifra. "The clues expect us to fill in the names of the different toes, the names of the different foot bones, the names of dancers and football players who use fancy footwork, and, of course, the famous book by Dr. Seuss. We can work on it together and after our hour is finished, you can do it with anyone else!"

Just then, the officer returned. "What's the name of the holiday you are all celebrating?" he asked.

Leah stood up and smiled. "It's Pesach or Passover. It's the story of the Exodus from Egypt."

"It must be a holiday with a lot of partying. I know that you have a special nighttime meal ... and now this special day at the park! It sounds like it's fun to be a Jew."

"It's not just a matter of fun and games; we have special commandments that we must obey," she replied. "But today is one of the Intermediate Days of the holiday, and we are permitted to take pleasure trips like this one."

"Well, strange things are happening," he mused. "A woman just came to me and told me that her daughter's change of clothing, a pink smock, is missing. She brought along extra clothes for her preschooler because she can get wet and dirty here in the park. The clothing was in their stroller, and now it's gone!"

"The stroller?" asked Rachel

"Nope. The smock," laughed Officer Daniel. "It's just like the wig that the other woman reported...." He decided to change the subject. "Did you see that black Lincoln that pulled up to the entrance of the park? Do you know whose car that was?"

She turned to look directly at him. "No, I don't. Do you?"

The police officer shook his head. He looked skeptical. "I figured that the owner is one of your VIPs," he said, spelling out the letters, "and you would recognize him."

"What's a VIP?" asked Rachel impatiently.

"A 'very important person.'" Officer Daniel replied. "Well, he sure must be a rich one."

After he walked away, the girls began talking about school. Rachel sighed and shifted position on the bench. "You know how Morah Zimmerman was explaining to us about the Oleh Regel, the three-times-a-year trip to Jerusalem to the Bais HaMikdash?"

"The three times are the Yomim Tovim of Succos in the fall and Pesach and Shavuos in the spring," nodded Shifra.

"Well," continued Rachel. "Do you remember that last year around Shavuos, I twisted my other ankle while picking flowers?"

"Yeah!" agreed Shifra. "Sure I remember that! You were also stung by a bee and your arm swelled, too. I think your arm looked worse than your ankle!" She laughed and continued, "And before Sukkos, when your brother was building the family sukkah, a board fell over and hit your knee. After that you couldn't go apple-picking with us on Chol Hamoed Sukkos."

Suddenly their conversation was interrupted by shouts and cries. The girls turned and watched the woman who had previously alighted from the Lincoln Continental rushing toward the main entrance. She was in a panic and screaming for the police.

Officer Daniel stepped out of the main office. "Calm down, lady, and tell me what happened. What's the matter?" he asked.

"My son has been kidnapped!" she shouted

"What makes you think so? Maybe he's just lost in the park," the officer responded calmly.

"My Mendy went on the carousel and he wasn't on his horse when the ride ended. I looked for him and I couldn't find him. It's your fault," she pointed angrily at Officer Daniel. "My driver was supposed to come into the park with us and help me with Mendy, but you wouldn't let him park the car. You claimed it was a No Parking Zone, and we couldn't leave the car there. He had to look for parking and he still has not come back."

"Maybe your son got off himself and went to a different ride," suggested Officer Daniel. Meanwhile he was also talking into his walkie-talkie, calling for other park personnel to begin looking for the child. "Give me the boy's description," he said to the mother, "and we'll make an announcement over the P.A. system so everyone in the park will help look for him."

Mendy's mother was not appeased. She began wailing again and screaming, "Mendy! Mendy! Where are you?"

Suddenly the chauffer ran up to her. He had finally parked in a distant area of the parking lot. He completed a call on his cell phone as he ran, and then turned accusingly to Officer Daniel. "Mr. Pincus is on his way here with your commander. We were afraid that this could happen because Mr. Pincus is a well-known philanthropist. The family was advised to keep Mendy at home because of kidnapping threats, but Mendy cried so much, begging to go to the park on Chol HaMoed Pesach. Now look what's happened! Because I was not there to protect him, someone has taken Mendy. It's your fault! You didn't believe me when I told you I was a bodyguard as well as a chauffeur!"

Officer Daniel looked stunned. He tried to stay calm but he was very upset. "Don't blame me! You should have parked in the lot like everyone else and then accompanied the kid from there! Give me a picture of Mendy and we will search the grounds for him," he said.

Mendy's mother looked ready to collapse. She stared at the officer. Her driver spoke to her quietly and offered her water from Leah's bottle.

Nervously, Mrs. Pincus slid her bag from her shoulder and looked inside. She found a picture of Mendy and handed it to Officer Daniel.

"I want copies of this picture distributed immediately," he said as he turned to one of the park guards who had come running at his radioed summons. "Quick, make 100 copies and pass them out to all our officers and all park personnel."

Leah was quietly listening to all the excitement around her. She was thinking and the look on her face showed that she was concentrating deeply. She tapped her finger on her lip in her typical thoughtful style.

"Leah," said Rachel, "shall I tell the officer who you are?"

Leah didn't hear her friend's words. Unexpectedly, tears came to her eyes. She rubbed her eyes with the back of her hand and a determined look crossed her face. "Officer Daniel," she called as she stood up and walked over to him.

"I'm sorry, young lady," he started, "but we are busy now. I don't have time to chat with you."

She cleared her throat and continued talking. "I don't think that Mendy has been taken out of the park yet," she jumped right in. "There hasn't been enough time for that."

He stared at her. "That makes sense," he said seriously.

"But the kidnapper *will* try to get him out as soon as possible. You must immediately close all entrances and exits except this main one. No one should be permitted to leave the park from any other exit."

He stared at her and nodded. He called over one of his men and gave him the new orders. "And then what?" he asked her.

Leah wiped her eyes and said flatly. "Mendy's mother should stand near this exit and watch the feet of every child who leaves here."

Officer Daniel stared at her and began making notes. He looked anxious. "Why the feet?" he asked.

"If someone tries to sneak Mendy out of the park, they will have to change the way he looks. They probably will change his clothing. As a four-year-old, he is capable of walking out of park on his own feet. Well, the shoes of a child who can walk would have to fit him. So, they will not be able to change his shoes, even if they change his clothes," said Leah. After a moment she added, half to herself, "This Yom Tov is one of the sholosh regalim. I feel that Hashem will make sure that they will keep his shoes on him."

Officer Daniel hesitated and spoke calmly. "We will continue our search for him in the park, just in case the kidnappers are frightened off by our announcements, and decide to leave him somewhere in the park."

Mrs. Pincus was called over. Officer Daniel explained Leah's theory to her and escorted her to an alcove near the entrance of the park, from which she could see the gates but not be seen by the passersby. He advised her to watch for every child leaving the park. "Don't look only at the faces of the children," he reminded her. "Concentrate on the shoes!"

After about an hour, a man and woman approached the exit with their little blonde daughter, who seemed to be sleeping on her mother's shoulder.

Suddenly Mendy's mother looked startled and began to scream. "Mendel! Mendele!" she called. The child in the pink smock moved her head in response to the call and a blond wig fell off. The child looked both sleepy and frightened. It was immediately obvious that the "little girl" was hide the fact that he was a boy. The officers grabbed the kidnappers and waved victoriously at Office Daniel and Mrs. Pincus.

Mendy's mother ran toward her son. "Mendele, Mendele," she sobbed. The security guards let her through as she grabbed her son and held him. The man and woman were taken away by the State Police, who had been called in earlier ... and just then, Mendy's father showed up with the police captain. They shook Officer Daniel's hand and thanked him. He blushed and looked at Leah.

Leah shook her head. She did not want anyone to know that she had helped rescue the child. For her, it was enough satisfaction to know a Jewish boy had been saved from terrible people and a terrible fate.

Rachel and Shifra smiled happily. Rachel said that the mystery had been solved only because she had hurt her foot. Now she knew why Hashem had wanted her to fall — it was so that Leah would be available to save Mendy.

Shifra shook her head. "No," she said. "Hashem wanted Leah to teach us the importance of regolim — using our feet. They can lead us one way or the other ... and we should always take care of them and use them to do the mitzvos of Hashem."

Leah looked at things from a slightly different perspective. "Everything happens because of Hashem. We must daven that only good happens to all of us."

A Mystery From Afar

A Shavuos Mystery

Leah Lamdan was sprawled on the floor near her friend Rachel. The two of them were in the process of making a chart about the lives of our Avos according to the commentaries of Rashi and others. A large oak-tag chart was leaning against one of the dresser drawers. Printed on the top of the chart with a blue marker were the Hebrew words, "*Maaseh Avos Siman LeVonim*," which is usually translated to mean, "Our fathers' deeds are a sign for their children." The Hebrew name of the parashah from which they drew their information about each tzaddik was written in green in the first column. The name of each *Av* was written in the next column, with similarities and differences carefully noted, and the sentences or pesukim describing them written alongside. Leah sighed and gathered more papers and a booklet from her desk.

At that moment the girls were immersed in Parshas VaYetzei and were learning about Yaakov Avinu and his dream of the angels moving up and down the ladder leading to Heaven. The girls were so engrossed in what they were doing that they did not hear Rabbi Lamdan knocking on the open door. Rabbi Lamdan paused in the doorway, head tilted as he listened to them talking to each other. He cleared his throat and again knocked on the door. Leah looked up, delighted to see him standing there.

Rabbi Lamdan wore an amused expression. "You have a very interesting way of learning Torah," he commented. Leah was sitting on the floor, leaning over toward the chart. A pencil protruded from her mouth and another one was tucked behind her ear. Rachel held a marker nonchalantly in her hand as she balanced a ruler between her fingers. She was cocooned among soft, cuddly, stuffed animals that were strewn across the floor. Rabbi Lamdan shook his head. He looked sideways at the chart near the dresser. "I didn't mean to disturb you. Are you inventorying something? Do you need some help? If you want, I can get you an easel that you can lean your chart against. That may be more comfortable than what you are doing now."

Leah shook her head and shrugged. She experienced a jumble of emotions. Amusement — because her father had seen them in such an unconventional way and shame — because her father had seen them in such an unconventional way

"Thanks," she said softly, "but we are almost finished for the evening. We are both exhausted and this parashah is not an easy one to understand."

"It looks like an interesting presentation," Rabbi Lamdan continued. "It seems quite analytical."

Rachel's smile was really awe-inspiringly dazzling. Until that moment, Leah had thought that the description, "lights up a face" was just an expression. Now, as she stared at her friend, she fully appreciated the phrase for the first time.

"Are you really finishing up?" he asked, gesturing toward his study. His brow was furrowed and he clasped the back of his neck, as if to relieve tension there. He looked oddly troubled as he took a deep breath and raised his eyebrows. "There is a gentleman in my study with a peculiar problem," he said mildly. "Lieutenant McCarthy sent him here."

"Oh ... then," Leah said, "we are finished with this school project for this evening." She looked at Rachel, whose blue-eyed stare gazed at her in admiration. After a second, Leah broke visual contact with her and then half-turned toward her father. "Let's go," she said resolutely. She paused in the doorway, waiting for Rachel to join her. Rachel smiled, nodded, and sauntered off with her.

A short, stout man, wearing a small yarmulke that sat like an island on his bald pate, arose to greet them. In contrast to the top of his head, his face was heavily bearded, and his eyes were fiercely sharp.

"Mr. Lifshitz," Rabbi Lamdan made the introductions, "this is my daughter, Leah, and her friend, Rachel."

Mr. Lifshitz stepped toward them and then stopped as if waiting for someone else to speak. He stood silently for a moment and then folded his arms across his chest. "Leah," he said quietly. "I need your help."

Leah Lamdan asked grimly. "What's wrong? How can I help?"

Mr. Lifshitz retreated a few paces and sat down again. He gulped as his lips quivered. "It's about my brother," he rasped. There was silence for a moment. "I am afraid for him." His face turned pale with anxiety.

Rabbi Lamdan stepped toward a little refrigerator at the side of his desk. He bent down, opened it, and removed a bottle of water, immediately pouring some of the refreshing liquid into a cup on his desk. "Drink this," he urged Mr. Lifshitz. "It will be easier for you to speak."

"All right," he answered. He quickly recited the berachah, gulped down some water, and glanced at his watch. "It's been a long day."

Leah waited and watched the man carefully to better assess the situation. She felt that it was important to observe him quietly before hearing his story. A few moments later, Mr. Lifshitz cleared his throat and began to tell his story.

"My father, may he rest in peace, passed away almost two months ago. My mother, olehah hashalom, had passed away many years before. You should probably know that my father, zichrono livrachah, had emigrated from Israel many years ago. He was quite well off in Israel, and when he came to the United States, he started an enterprising business here. Less than two weeks ago, my brother Levi and I decided to clean out his apartment and donate many of his things to a charity in Israel. My brother had tickets to go there for Shavuos. While sorting out my father's clothing, Levi felt something in the lining of one of the suits. He saw that the lining had been opened up and resewn; we opened it again and, to our surprise, removed a map! The map looked very important. It seemed to be the map of a location in Eretz Yisrael, and actually pinpointed a treasure of some sort. Since my brother already had a ticket to go to Israel, we made a copy of the map so he could take it with him. He left five days ago and since that time I have not heard from him. It is not unusual that he hasn't called or written because ... well, because he just never did before. Yet, I know my brother. When he has something to tell me, he'll say it to my face."

Mr. Lifshitz took another sip of water. Talking seemed to drain his energy and it took a few more minutes before he was able to continue. It seemed that he might be reconsidering what he had come to say, but then he shrugged and continued.

"Last night, a stranger came to my house. He introduced himself as Mr. Josephy, from Israel. He is here in the United States for a few days on personal business, and tomorrow night he is returning to Eretz Yisrael to be there for Shavuos. He told me that he had met Levi on the plane and my brother had told him about our map. Mr. Josephy claims that Levi fell as he was leaving the airport and hurt his arm. When the accident happened, Levi compounded the problem by spilling some liquid on the map. The map is not legible as is, and he says that Levi would like me to make him another copy."

Leah frowned. She looked skeptical. "I don't understand," she said emphatically. "How can I help?"

Mr. Lifshitz grimaced. "Somehow there is something about Mr. Josephy that I don't trust. I don't have the expertise or patience or time to comb through his story. I just feel that it is not kosher and I am afraid for my brother. Maybe Mr. Josephy is telling me the truth and my brother wants me to send him another copy of the map. I am surprised by what he tells me," he paused," and I'm not sure that I believe him."

Rachel looked at her wristwatch. Tension seemed to fill the room. There was an overlong silence. "If you are afraid to give him the map, then don't," Rachel said.

"Your brother should have given him some kind of proof that they met and that he wants or needs another copy. Why should you trust the man merely on his say-so?"

Leah put her hand out and touched Rachel's shoulder, indicating that she should be quiet. Rachel inhaled sharply as she turned to look at her friend. Leah's pale face emphasized the strain in her eyes.

Leah turned to Mr. Lifshitz. "Do you think that your brother is being held against his will by Mr. Josephy? Is that what you are afraid of?"

"I don't know," he murmured back in response. "I just want to hear something from Levi himself." He stopped and looked at Leah in quiet despair. "I explained to your father that I made arrangement that Mr. Josephy should come here and describe the details to your father. This was not my original idea. Lieutenant McCarthy from the 66th Precinct made that suggestion. My family knows him from some previous problems we had, so I sought his advice. I thought that he might do a background check on Mr. Josephy, but there really isn't time if he plans to go back to Israel tomorrow night, as he told me."

Leah scowled. She looked quite uncomfortable. "How can we help?" she repeated. "What do you want us to do?"

"Mr. Josephy will be here any minute. I want you to observe him, to listen to what he says and how he presents it. I want you to tell me if he sounds legitimate."

Leah pursed her lips. She sounded dubious as she spoke. "How can I judge someone so quickly? We are advised in Pirkei Avos not to judge someone like that. I do not want the responsibility of making such a quick decision."

Mr. Lifshitz seemed to be a pathetic figure as he listened to her words. He looked around and shrugged, frowning sadly. When the doorbell rang his mouth twitched and his knuckles whitened as he twisted a handkerchief that he took from his pocket and used to wipe the back of his neck.

They heard Mrs. Lamdan calling out, "I'm coming," as she went to answer the door, while Leah moved toward a chair at the far end of the room, She then sat down and used that time to calm herself so she could marshal her thoughts about the situation.

Rachel frowned. She didn't know what to do. Should she stay or should she go? She glanced toward the door and thoughtfully looked at a stepstool placed in front of one of the large bookcases. She smiled at Leah and then sat down.

Mrs. Lamdan ushered the visitor into the study and hurried back with a tray of coffee and cookies. When Mr. Josephy entered the room, Leah was pleasantly surprised at the sight of the big, stocky, handsome man with sparse gray hair and a cleft chin. His concerned eyes seemed pouchy from lack of sleep. A small yarmulke was perched near the top of his head, just like that of Mr. Lifshitz.

After a gracious handshake with Rabbi Lamdan, he formally introduced himself. "The name is Josephy," he began as he set his briefcase down and smiled. Then he sat as his gray eyes assessed Rabbi Lamdan through a pair of chromium-rimmed glasses. Leah felt that she caught a hint of cruelty in the set of his mouth, but then supposed that could be just her reaction to the set of circumstances that had brought him to the Lamdans. Yet she felt that the hint grew more pronounced as he curled his lips, revealing unnaturally white and even teeth.

A chill settled on Leah's shoulders as she folded her hands on her lap and coolly observed him from the side.

She lifted her eyebrows a fraction as her father introduced the others in the room. Mr. Josephy turned and nodded as he glanced around the room.

"I didn't come here to cause any problems," he began sharply as he sat back in his chair and pulled out his business card. "I am here on a buying trip for my company and I thought I could do a fellow Jew a favor." He scowled and stared around with a gleam in his eye. Leah felt that he looked nervous and short-tempered.

Mr. Lifshitz frowned and glanced toward Rabbi Lamdan. "I am sorry to make this so difficult for you," he began, "but when I listened to your story, I became nervous for my brother's sake. He is not the type of person to tell his business to a total stranger."

Mr. Josephy blinked and the corners of his mouth quirked up. Then he took a cup of coffee from the tray Mrs. Lamdan had placed on the desk and began to sip slowly. He remained silent as his hand hovered over the cup and his gaze slid toward Leah. "You must excuse me, but I came here to show my willingness to help, and I cannot stay long."

"I apologize for this quick meeting," Rabbi Lamdan nodded as he began to consult some notes on his desk. His expression must have reflected his thoughts because he smiled gently and folded his hands on top of the notepad. "Mr. Lifshitz is quite nervous about the circumstances under which you met his brother and the fact that his brother has not contacted him at all since leaving for Israel."

"I explained to him already that his brother and I met on the plane, in the hotel, and finally even at the Bais Olam, the cemetery. At the Bais Olom, his brother wore a cast that covered his fingers and went up past his elbow. It was hot and cumbersome and he seemed agitated. I mentioned in passing that I was going back to the States for the week and he immediately flooded me with questions about myself and my business. I guess he wanted to ascertain if I was honest."

Leah shifted in her chair. Her eyes looked deeply shadowed and troubled. Mr. Josephy hesitated and went on as he put down the coffee cup and fingered it. He considered his words before he spoke. "We hit it off almost immediately," he said with pride. "It was almost sunset when we started talking to each other at the Bais Olom. We spoke at length about many things. As you can see from my business card, I am in investments and your brother felt that some of my ideas could be lucrative for him. When it finally became very dark and it was time to go, he asked me to contact his brother Moishe and tell him that he had accidentally ruined his copy of the map and that he wanted another one."

Mr. Lifshitz stared wonderingly at Rabbi Lamdan. "Why didn't he contact me? He could have written or called. A telephone call from Israel is not as expensive as it was years ago," he added.

Mr. Josephy clapped his hands and held them outwards. Abruptly he said, "You know your brother better than I do." He turned to stare at Leah, looking into her eyes. And what he saw there surprised him. His mouth pulled down ironically and after a moment, he lifted his coffee cup again and sipped its contents slowly.

"Well, if you don't want to give me the map, I shall leave. I have many other things to do today," He put down the cup and stood up. "You have my card. Let me know your decision."

Leah frowned. Apparently something was bothering her but she couldn't put her finger on it. She looked at Mr.

Lifshitz and grinned sheepishly. She reminded herself of something her father once told her. "When someone tells you something or does something that you are not sure about, look for the unusual even if the unusual seems to have nothing to do with the matter at hand."

Leah pressed a hand to her lips. In the silence that followed, she heard some traffic from the outside, sounding louder than normal. She swallowed and cleared her throat. And then, of course, what was bothering her suddenly caught her attention.

"Are you going to Eretz Yisrael for Shavuos?" she asked. "It must be a lovely time of the year. You know," she said apologetically, "my friend Rachel and I are doing some homework for school. We are reviewing *Parshas VaYetzei*, which begins with Yaakov's dream. Rashi asks a question on the pasuk that says that Yaakov rested and the sun went down. Doesn't it usually happen the other way round: the sun goes down and then a person rests? Rashi answers his own question by stating that the sun went down very quickly so that Yaakov would lie down at that spot. It was a special miracle, for the speed of the sun setting was much faster than usual." She held up her hand to forestall discussion.

"I remember learning that in Yerushalayim the sun sets quickly because Israel is close to the equator." She glanced toward her father. "That means that they could not have had a long discussion at the cemetery, because it gets dark too fast."

Rabbi Lamdan nodded his head knowingly. He was sitting in his chair, perfectly still, with his hands folded. It was as if he knew a secret that he was about to reveal. "Israel *is* close to the equator," repeated Rabbi Lamdan. His eyes shifted toward Mr. Josephy. He nodded slightly toward his guest. "The sun sets quickly in Eretz Yisrael. You can't have a long conversation from the time the sun is ready to set until it actually sets."

Mr. Josephy squinted and tried to act offended, then decided that it was time to leave. He wiped his hands on his jacket as the doorbell rang. Rabbi Lamdan focused his eyes on a monitor in the corner of the study. He then buzzed the door open and Lieutenant McCarthy joined them in the study.

◇◇◇

Later, Mr. Lifshitz returned with some information. He sounded relieved. He smiled at Rabbi Lamdan and Leah. "My brother called," he explained. "He did meet Mr. Josephy at the airport before getting on the plane. They actually sat next to each other during the flight. Just before landing, Mr. Josephy said that he was thirsty and would bring them both some water to drink. My brother said that he sipped a little of the water and it tasted bitter, so he really didn't finish the cup, but I guess he drank enough. They got off the plane together, went through Customs, and then to get their luggage. Suddenly Levi felt faint. He was hot and nauseated and he opened his jacket to cool down while breathing some fresh air. Mr. Josephy 'miraculously' had more water and gave him some. Levi remembers suddenly feeling that he was falling and spilling his drink all over his jacket and shirt. And that is all he remembered. He woke up in a motel. He was alone and he could not find the map!

"Luckily, after being questioned by Lieutenant McCarthy, our 'friend' Josephy admitted drugging Levi and trying to steal the map. His own water had ruined the copy, and that's why he came here to try to get one from me. The lieutenant told him that he was lucky I didn't press charges — but Josephy doesn't know that Levi is waiting for him in Eretz Yisrael with the Israeli police! After all, there's a 'small matter' of assault and kidnapping waiting for him there!"

THE CRIMSON ATARAH

A ROSH CHODESH MYSTERY

CHAPTER 1

DANGER IN THE SNOW

Swirls of heavy snowflakes driven by gusty winds whistled across the vast expanse of John F. Kennedy International Airport in Queens, New York. The snow dashed against the big picture window in the upstairs arrivals lounge and spiraled back into the murky whiteness of the winter morning. Inside the lounge, Rabbi Avraham Lamdan and his daughter Leah sat on leather armchairs, watching and waiting for Dodah Devorah, Mrs. Lamdan's sister, who lived in Paris. Her flight from London was due at any moment.

"Of all the luck!" Leah shook her head in despair. "This must be the worst winter we've had in years." She tucked a strand of hair in place and shuddered. "B-r-r-r, and I do mean b-r-r-r!"

"They say the plane is scheduled to land on time. I hope the instruments really can see through this snow." Rabbi Lamdan's face looked worried and tired. "Your aunt has suffered so much in the past five years. I can't imagine how difficult it must be for her to come to New York now."

"Please, Abba," Leah stood up and glanced at the pattern of snow swirling up against the wide window. They were in the VIP waiting lounge, waiting for Dodah Devorah, who always traveled first class. "Dodah Devorah wanted to come. After all, Ima will be laid up in that cast for at least six weeks. Ima and her sister haven't seen each other for such a long time. Even in these trying circumstances, I think their get-together is a wonderful idea." She looked over her shoulder at her father as she spoke.

◇◇◇

While running for a bus, Mrs. Lamdan had slipped, fallen, and broken her leg. It was now in a full-length cast, and that would not be easy for a busy and active woman like Mrs. Lamdan. Aside from her job as the regular substitute teacher in Bais Malkah Elementary School, she was on many active committees to help the needy, the physically disadvantaged, and special-needs children, as well as a vital member of the Bikur Cholim and Oseh Chesed Societies. How could she manage all that while laid up?

"I'll teach you what half the knowledgeable world today knows," her sister had offered during a phone call to the convalescent. "I'll teach you how to use a computer; once you learn to use it you'll never understand how you managed without it!"

"I don't even own a computer," Sarah Lamdan had shaken her head in disbelief.

"That's no problem," her sister had replied. The family in New York could imagine the high, righteous arch of Dodah Devorah's eyebrow as she jerked her head upward in order to arouse a swell of courage. "I'll get you one as soon as I arrive," and then with undeterred single-mindedness Devorah repeated. "I am coming, Sis. I'm taking a plane to America and I'll arrange everything you need!"

Mrs. Lamdan had smiled. "I really wanted to help *you* after all the pain and suffering you've gone through. But now you're coming to help me! The world turns and turns, and everything changes."

"Please, Sis," Devorah cried excitedly, "we'll help each other! I'll teach you how to use the computer and you'll teach me how to accept nisyonos with emunah and bitachon."

◇◇◇

Now Leah and her father were waiting in the lounge for Dodah Devorah's arrival. Rabbi Lamdan was about to get up when the arrivals board lit up.

"I'll get a luggage cart," he told Leah, "so we won't have to carry the suitcases and packages." Leah had a great fondness for her dodah, who was fun and lively company and had a giving and warm heart. Just anticipating her aunt's arrival, Leah's own heart beat faster. She remembered once talking to her aunt about one of the mysteries she had been trying to solve. Dodah Devorah had been fascinated by Leah's application of Torah knowledge to help solve the mystery.

"You must keep a written record of your mysteries," she had told her, "because they could be good examples for others to learn and live by. I think that I, too, would be very interested in reading your stories." Leah had laughed when her aunt made that suggestion, but afterwards she thought that it really wasn't a bad idea at all! She couldn't wait to show Dodah Devorah what she had written so far.

Time seemed to pass very slowly as Leah waited through an excruciating silence. Suddenly, there she was! The doors opened and Dodah Devorah emerged. She looked older than Leah remembered her because her dark sheitel was done up in a chignon instead of flowing to her shoulders, but the big smile on her face when she saw Leah was the same. It seemed to take away some of the sadness around her eyes. Leah ran to her and hugged her excitedly. Dodah Devorah then stepped back and appraised her niece.

"You've changed," she said to her. "You seem more poised. I remember you used to be shy."

Leah grinned and motioned to Rabbi Lamdan who was moving forward with a cart. Tears glistened in Dodah Devorah's blue eyes.

"I was hoping that the next time I saw my sister would be at a joyous occasion. How does Sarah feel? Can she get around?"

Rabbi Lamdan smiled. "You know your sister. She's trying to figure out how she can get around without being mobile."

"That's easy!" Dodah Devorah smiled mischievously. "We live in an age when one can get around just by pressing buttons."

As they stepped outside toward the parking lot, the wind blowing across the huge airfield carried the crisp, cold bite of winter, and snowdrifts continued to pile up against the heavy fences surrounding the parking lot.

"Let's go," Rabbi Lamdan said crisply. "It will not be easy traveling home in this weather."

"How was the flight?" Leah asked her aunt as she pressed her hat down and pushed her fingers into her gloves.

"It was a good flight and it even made me feel good." Dodah Devorah said, and then immediately added, "There is a wedding in New York tonight. Many Jewish Londoners were on the plane."

"They traveled in this weather?" Leah asked in amazement. "I hope they get to the wedding hall safely."

"Lots of people planned on going to this wedding," her aunt nodded. She continued speaking. "The plane was booked solid. There was a gentleman at the sales counter urgently trying to get a ticket on our flight. He was arguing with the airline personnel but they told him that there was nothing available. Actually, there was one seat still available in first class but Mr. Klein, the gentleman I saw, had only cash with him and not enough for a first-class ticket. He had no credit card and no bank card."

She looked around and tried to get her bearings as they walked toward the parking lot.

"I didn't realize that there are still people who prefer to use cash when making big purchases," Leah stated. "After all, traveling from London to New York is not cheap. How could the man leave his house without a credit card?"

Dodah Devorah nodded in agreement. She consulted a small pad that she carried in her coat pocket. "I always carry my credit card with me, so I offered Mr. Klein a first-class ticket."

"You offered to pay for a first-class ticket just like that?" Leah asked in amazement as she tried to snap her fingers in their thick gloves.

Dodah Devorah laughed and gave her niece a squeeze. "Mr. Klein was carrying a Sefer Tehillim. I knew I could trust him. I felt that helping another person is just an added zchus. Mr. Klein was quite embarrassed and offered me a list of references. He gave me the cash that he had with him, and he wanted to arrange a method for me to pick up the rest of the money. I told him to do me a favor and give it to a worthy cause — to any charity that he felt deserves it."

Leah smiled. The ease in which her aunt always did things amazed her. "So what happened then?" she asked softly as she stared wide-eyed at her aunt.

Dodah Devorah sighed as she slipped her arm around Leah's waist. Then she brightened up. "Well, he offered to bless me because, after all, Mr. Klein is a kohen," she pointed out. "I asked him to reserve a blessing for my sister, your mother, who was recuperating from a mishap and needed a quick recovery. He blessed your mother and now I feel confident that soon she will be running around as usual." She breathed a sigh of relief as she eyed her niece with interest.

"Did he bless you also?" Leah asked incredulously as she searched her aunt's face to see if she was pulling her leg. The weather conditions were getting worse and Leah began to cough.

Dodah Devorah inhaled deeply and patted her heart. "Yes. He blessed both of us. I would never turn down a berachah from a fellow Jew. A berachah is always a plus."

Leah smiled and shivered a little. She was becoming excited in spite of herself. She hummed a few notes to herself and then shyly asked, "Did he sit next to you on the flight?"

"Not at all," her aunt stated emphatically. "I sat next to a total stranger. I really had to rethink some business deals I have to contend with, so I didn't mind the quiet. But the quiet didn't last." She looked wistful as she continued, "Mr. Klein wanted to daven Shacharis. It seems that he had received some kind of emergency call at home in the morning and he had been advised to leave London as soon as possible. He did not have the chance to daven before he left his house and he realized at the airport that he needed a minyan to recite the Kaddish, because it was the yahrzeit of a close relative. So after purchasing his ticket and getting on the plane he put on his tallis and tried to find a minyan. He looked like a ghost as he walked down the economy-class aisle. The steward stopped him, and held him back, but Mr. Klein was so excited that he couldn't explain himself. I could hear him from my seat, and, just listening to the few words he stuttered, I understood the situation and explained it to the steward." She fidgeted with her fingers and Leah sensed that she was thinking about something else. She had that quizzical look in her eye.

"Did he return to first class afterwards?"

"Oh yes. He passed by my seat and thanked me again for everything. I felt a little awkward," she laughed. "The man sitting next to me was fascinated by Mr. Klein's tallis. He asked Mr. Klein why it had no atarah. I was surprised. I didn't even think that the man next to me was Jewish! How did he know about atarahs? He saw the look on my face and guessed what I was thinking.

"'I'm not Jewish,' he said, 'but I deal with buying and selling Jewish artifacts.' Mr. Klein mumbled something and returned to his seat. He looked embarrassed to be talking to us. He looked to me as if he wanted to cover his face and sink down." Dodah Devorah smiled broadly.

"Mr. Klein may have felt sheepish and uncomfortable, but I was already interested in my seatmate's vocation. A non-Jew who buys and sells Jewish artifacts! How surprising! I informed my seatmate that I had a beautiful atarah on my husband's tallis at home." He looked quite impressed.

"'It must be beautiful,' he said. 'Your husband must be very pleased, for I can tell that you are a woman of impeccable taste.' I appreciated his thoughts and sighed. He heard my sadness. I don't know what came over me then. I'm usually not so talkative, especially to a stranger," Dodah Devorah continued.

Leah gave her aunt her full attention as she attempted to smile. But Dodah Devorah's face seemed strained and she stared ahead without looking at her niece. She gazed past her. Her usual cheerful vivacity seemed to have flown. There was something different in her eyes, a need Leah hadn't seen before.

Dodah Devorah continued her story. "'My husband died before he ever had a chance to wear the beautiful atarah. I bought it for him, but it could not be buried with him,' I told my seatmate."

Leah did not say anything. She merely nodded. Her aunt seemed like a soldier debriefing after a battle. Once begun, it was difficult to stop her, so Leah didn't try. Dodah Devorah shook her head slowly. Her face looked stiff. She put her hands together, growing earnest. "He looked baffled, as if he didn't know what to say. And then he gave me his business card," she said slowly. "'I am willing to buy your atarah sight unseen at any price you ask,' he said to me. 'I trust your instinct and taste. It is probably a beautiful atarah.'"

Leah raised an eyebrow in a silent question. Dodah Devorah looked away from her. There was a pained silence and then after a minute she added solemnly. "'That atarah is my link to Hersh. I cannot give it up,' I told him. I was not pleased with his reply. He said, 'Your husband would want you to relinquish it by giving it to someone else.' I repeated that I would not sell it," she said resolutely. "'You have my card,' he answered. 'Call me anytime; I will remember you.'" Dodah Devorah smiled but there was sadness in it. Her smile quickly disappeared as she held the card toward Leah. It was imprinted, "Mr. S. Bishop — Gold, Jewelry, Jewish Artifacts." Dodah Devorah frowned.

"It was the strangest thing," she continued. "When I finally got my suitcase after we landed, I looked for both Mr. Klein and Mr. Bishop. Both seemed to have disappeared."

They had almost reached the parking lot. Leah heard a squeal of tires as a car tore out of the parking lot and passed by very close to them. Dodah Devorah, Rabbi Lamdan, and Leah exchanged terrified glances. That was when Leah saw him — an older man, standing alone. He looked frightened as he stood nearby, wearing an overcoat and clutching a violin case in his hands. He turned and faced them as they neared him. The eyes in his worn face were tired and pleading. Rabbi Lamdan stopped for a moment and said in a low, deep-toned, and resonant voice, "Reb Yid? May I help you?"

Nervously, in a soft Yiddish accent with an almost indiscernible lisp, the stranger answered, "Shema Yisrael! Ich muz gein tzu Boro Park [I must go to Boro Park]!" He then took off his glasses with an anxious gesture and rubbed his eyes. His face looked drawn and haggard, and worry wrinkles creased the skin around his eyes.

Rabbi Lamdan smiled "It's on our way," he said. "Is that all your luggage?"

The old man nodded, looking hesitantly from Dodah Devorah to Leah and back to Rabbi Lamdan. "If it's no bother," he sighed. "Otherwise, I'll wait for the bus to take to the train."

"I won't hear of it," Rabbi Lamdan shook his head. "You would be doing me a favor by joining us in the car. It is so windy that more people and luggage in the car will help weigh it down, which, I hope, means less chance of skidding. The roads are treacherous. Wait here and I'll bring the car over." He hurried away with the luggage and Leah and Dodah Devorah stood near the old man, waiting for Rabbi Lamdan's return.

"Where are you from?" Dodah Devorah asked curiously.

"I am coming from Boston," was the reply. "I went to visit my son —" and he abruptly stopped talking and turned his face aside.

Dodah Devorah eyed Leah thoughtfully before speaking to her. "Your Uncle Hersh and I once stayed in Boston. They have some very good hospitals there —" and then she too stopped in mid-sentence and stared out toward the highway.

"Here comes Abba," shouted Leah over the sound of the wind as Rabbi Lamdan approached them in the family car. Leah and Dodah Devorah climbed into the back seat as Rabbi Lamdan leaned over and opened the front passenger door.

"Reb Yid," he said, "Get in."

The old man smiled nervously as he pulled his violin case across his body and got into the car. In shifting his grip, he almost dropped the violin case.

"*Oy vey!*" he shouted in horror and then became silent.

Leah's father extended his arm for a handshake. "Avraham Lamdan is the name," he introduced himself.

"Mr. Shimon Brenner," was the sheepish reply.

"Where in Boro Park are you going?" asked Rabbi Lamdan.

There was a thoughtful pause. "I wish to go to Thirteenth Avenue and Fifty-Third Street," Mr. Brenner murmured lamely. He turned pale and shuddered every time clouds of snow hit the front window.

"Is that where you live?" Rabbi Lamdan asked with a smile.

"I guess that when I am in Brooklyn, that is my address; but it is not my home. It is my nephew's home. His name is Ari Brenner." The old man sighed again. He looked somewhat uncomfortable. He looked sad, too. "He is my late brother's son. I just hope that he got the message that I'm coming. Someone was supposed to call him and tell him I was leaving Boston earlier than expected. I tried calling from the airport, but there was no answer. I walked from my terminal to the next, thinking I would give him more time to come home from wherever he is."

"You mean he may not be home?" Rabbi Lamdan was disturbed.

Dodah Devorah's eyes narrowed slightly. "Perhaps he is on his way to the airport to pick you up," she interjected.

"No! No!" Mr. Brenner shrugged. "He doesn't drive. I always take a bus and a train when I come in." He spoke in a low tone.

Rabbi Lamdan grimaced. "I don't understand. When did you last speak to your nephew?" he asked.

"Last week," Mr. Brenner answered cautiously. "I called from my son's place and told him that I would be coming in one week earlier than expected." Then the old man shuddered and rubbed his hands again as he looked out the window. He looked carsick. The snow was still coming down heavily. Apprehensively Leah leaned back in the car and waited for other bits of information to be forthcoming but Mr. Brenner remained silent. Various questions occurred to Leah, and she fretted over the puzzle.

"Do you play the violin?" Rabbi Lamdan asked after a few minutes of silence. They were moving slowly on the highway although the road had not really iced up as yet.

"I used to play the violin a very long time ago," Shimon Brenner sighed. "I am a jeweler ... really a goldsmith ... by profession. I design gold jewelry, but business has not been good at all lately."

"Times aren't easy," admitted Rabbi Lamdan. "We can only pray that things will get better."

"Does your son play the violin?" Dodah Devorah leaned closer to the front from her seat in the back to ask the question.

"My son?" Shimon Brenner seemed thunderstruck. He stared back at Dodah Devorah. "My son?" he repeated and shook his head sadly. "My son just gets older." He took a deep breath and it seemed as if he were choking.

Leah made a quick, spontaneous movement forward. "Are you all right? Are you all right?" she repeated.

Mr. Brenner seemed momentarily embarrassed. He gave her an enigmatic glance and then nodded absently and shifted his gaze to the falling snow.

Dodah Devorah had the air of a take-charge person. "Do you want us to pull over to the side of the road?" she asked in a most decisive voice.

"No! No!" Mr. Brenner quavered. He winced and coughed and then cleared his throat. "I appreciate the lift. I'm just tired and anxious to get to Ari," he admitted.

Dodah Devorah gave her slight deprecating cough. "Sometimes family relationships are not easy to explain to strangers. You do believe that your nephew is home, don't you?" she inquired.

"I don't know. I assume that in this weather he must be home. Where else could he be?" he asked.

The same question flashed through Leah's mind. An inexplicable feeling of fear touched Leah. She gave a quick little shiver as her eyes fixed attentively on the back of Mr. Brenner's head.

After a short silence Rabbi Lamdan gestured to his seat-mate. "You'll ring the doorbell and we'll wait for you to go inside," he offered. At first there was silence and Leah's heart jumped with excitement. But then the wind rose to a howl and it was difficult to hear the response.

"That won't be necessary. I have a key." Shimon Brenner lifted his hand cautiously, waved a key, and smiled tremulously.

Rabbi Lamdan gave a short laugh. "Well," he said, "we're almost there." In less than ten minutes they were on Thirteenth Avenue.

"Leave me at the corner," said Mr. Brenner. "Ari's home is only one house off the corner. Otherwise, you'll have to drive around the block, since it's a one-way street."

Rabbi Lamdan stopped at the corner and looked around. Leah followed his gaze and saw that the streets were empty. "You must walk carefully," her father said as he scanned the snowy street, "it is quite slippery outside."

Mr. Brenner smiled back nervously. "Thank you again, tizku l'mitzvos," He leaned over and shook Rabbi Lamdan's extended hand.

"Wait!" Rabbi Lamdan gave Leah a fleeting glance as he pulled a card out of his inner coat-pocket. "My card," he said as he handed it to Mr. Brenner. "I'll, G-d willing, inquire in shul tomorrow if anyone needs a goldsmith. Please call me."

The wind suddenly died down and in the eerie silence they waited for a reply. Mr. Brenner nodded his head and pulled the collar of his coat upward, tighter around his neck. "Thank you, thank you," he said as he pulled his violin case out of the car and slammed the door. They watched him make his way toward the house and then, when they could not see him anymore, Rabbi Lamdan drove off.

CHAPTER 2

THE MISSING PATIENT

The streets had become quite icy, and at one point Rabbi Lamdan had to ease off on the gas to let a car pass him on the right. Then he moved over to the slow lane and lowered his speed even more until he finally stopped in front of his house. It had taken them all of 20 minutes. They stepped out of the car and walked lightly over the snow into the house. The house was comfortably warm and smelled delicious. Leah licked her lips and twitched her nose as she tried to decipher the aromas and guess what was cooking.

Sarah Lamdan greeted and hugged her sister, welcoming her to the United States. Mrs. Lamdan was sitting up on a bed in the living room. The two sisters held on to each other for a long minute and didn't talk. Finally, Leah's mother straightened up and wiped her eyes.

"These are my temporary quarters until I am allowed to walk. The doctors want me off the leg for the next five days," she explained. "But for six weeks, my leg will be in this cast. The doctors don't want me to exert myself and irritate the fracture."

Rabbi Lamdan brought a tray of hot tea into the living room. Dodah Devorah sipped her cup slowly.

"Ah!" she said. "This is good. It's so cold out there that this just hits the spot."

Leah brought out some cake, but Dodah Devorah shook her head. Her blue eyes widened slightly. "I drink my tea plain," she said, "just to savor the flavor." She sat down on the arm of a chair. From the way that they grinned at each other it was obvious that the two sisters were happy to see each other.

"I'll put your suitcases in my room," Leah said quite softly.

"Thank you, Leah," nodded her aunt as Leah bustled away. The two sisters were talking to each other as Leah returned to the living room. She listened to them coax and cajole each other as they talked about inconsequential things rather than discuss the reason for the trip.

After a while Leah caught her breath and stifled a yawn. "I'm sorry," she excused herself, "but I'm going to bed."

The excitement of the day had made Leah pleasantly tired. She dropped off to sleep almost as soon as her head touched the cool pillow. And her dreams were filled with visions of her mother and aunt as young girls. She didn't hear her aunt come into her room and go to sleep. She didn't see her aunt look out the window and glance briefly up and down the street. She didn't hear her sigh. About 4 a.m. Leah thought she heard the sound of a telephone ringing. She looked at the display on her clock and fell asleep again. Someone had answered the phone but Leah did not know it then.

In the morning she quietly tiptoed out of the room with her clothes over her arm so as not to awaken her aunt. She dressed and then looked out the window. How the weather had changed! The sun was beaming down and trying to melt the sheets of snow which were already marked with footprints. Slush abounded near the sidewalks as the sanitation trucks with their big shovels moved the icy slush to the curbs.

Looks better than I expected ..., she mused.

Her father had already returned from shul and was drinking a cup of hot coffee. Leah helped herself to a bowl of hot oatmeal cereal.

"We got a call last night from Maimonides Hospital," Rabbi Lamdan said as he moved a plate of cookies farther from his place setting.

"Maimonides Hospital?" She looked questioningly at him.

"Shimon Brenner was found last night, half-frozen. I guess his nephew was not home and he couldn't get into the house as he had expected. I don't know what happened to his key. He must have waited outside for his nephew to return but the weather was really too cold to stay outdoors. A police patrol found him huddled in the corner of the house, next to a garbage can. They took him to Maimonides."

Leah's face registered shock. "Oh the poor man!" she said. "What a terrible night to be out in the cold!" she frowned worriedly.

Her father continued the story. "Initially, they found his passport in his overcoat, so they were able to identify him by name. They also found my card with my phone number. So they called here about 4 o'clock in the morning.

There was nothing I could do at that hour. They wanted to keep him in the hospital overnight for observation, so I gave them what little information I had, and went back to sleep."

"How is he now?" Leah asked her father with concern. A worried look spread over her face. "Is there something we can do?"

"I understand that he's all right. He raised a ruckus when he woke up this morning. He protested that he did not want to be a nuisance and wanted to go home." Rabbi Lamdan smiled understandingly as he stirred his coffee. "I'm going to the hospital now. Would you like to join me?" he asked.

Leah digested this startling news. She was convinced that there was more to it than her father let on. "Yes," she said tensely. "Let's go."

The roads were slick as they passed a couple of fender benders on the way to the hospital. Rabbi Lamdan drove up and down the side streets to find a parking space. It was more difficult than usual because of the weather and parking was prohibited on the streets that were designated as snow routes. They finally found a parking spot four blocks from the hospital. They got out of the car and walked carefully toward the hospital.

They entered the waiting room and Rabbi Lamdan immediately strode over to the front desk. Leah was right behind him.

"Leah? Rabbi Lamdan?" a familiar voice suddenly called from across the waiting room. The man behind the voice marched over to her and her father.

"Lieutenant!" they said in unison. Heavyset Lieutenant McCarthy of the NYPD knew the Lamdans as his precinct's mystery-solvers. He was happy to see his friends.

His lips curved into a genuine smile as he rubbed his cheek gingerly. Then a self-conscious silence settled over them.

"What brings you both here so bright and early? Is Mrs. Lamdan all right?" he asked as he looked at each of them in turn.

"We're visiting a friend, Lieutenant," Rabbi Lamdan explained. "Mrs. Lamdan feels much better, thank you," he continued, glancing briefly at Leah. "Why are you here? I hope no one *you* know is hurt."

For a couple of seconds the lieutenant's expression was blank and then he snapped his fingers. "A policeman's job is never done," he started and then, "but since you are here ..." he grinned at them, "I could use your help." He glanced around. He had their attention, although Rabbi Lamdan was beginning to look impatient.

"In what way?" Rabbi Lamdan asked.

"I'm here to see an old man who, the nurses claim, speaks primarily Yiddish. I need an interpreter. We found him last night half-frozen in the snow."

Leah gasped. "Mr. Brenner," she said aloud. She shivered with excitement.

Lieutenant McCarthy stared at her in astonishment. Rabbi Lamdan cleared his throat.

"We are also here to see Mr. Brenner," he said quietly. "We met him yesterday at the airport. I drove him to his nephew's house. Obviously he never got into the building. But why is it a police matter?"

Lieutenant McCarthy shook his head. He moved forward and signaled Rabbi Lamdan and Leah to follow him into a small cubicle near the social worker's station. Lieutenant McCarthy then pointed to a violin case. Rabbi Lamdan frowned.

"Yes. I remember the violin case. It belongs to Mr. Brenner," he said. "Why isn't it in his room? Why do you have it?"

"We opened it to find out some information about the man we called 'the ice man.' We thought that maybe we would find a phone number of someone to contact. Instead, look at what we found!" He opened the old violin case and removed a badly folded tallis. "There are eight of these religious sheets in this case. Why does one man need so many? They aren't new; you can see that they have all been worn."

"Eight tallesim!" Rabbi Lamdan gawked. "Where is the violin?"

"No violin!" repeated the Lieutenant. "Only eight tal — tal, what you said."

"What did Mr. Brenner say? I'm sure that you must have asked him about the tallesim."

"He's been sleeping all this time. I haven't been able to ask him anything yet. But, I just got a message from the floor nurse. She says that he is awake now and he's complaining and stating that he wants to get out of here. So I have to go upstairs immediately and ask him my questions. But first, I want to examine these sheets ... uh, tallesim?"

Leah smiled faintly. Rabbi Lamdan rubbed his beard uncertainly. "How do you want me to help you?" he asked in a low tone.

"Well, Rabbi, you can tell me if these tallesim are kosher."

Rabbi Lamdan shrugged and nodded his head. "I would be very happy to help you," he said, "but Leah must get to school. She wanted to visit Mr. Brenner, too. So perhaps she can go upstairs first and speak to him. She may be able to pave the way for us and let him know that we are coming. He may be frightened if he first sees a man in a policeman's uniform."

"Sure," responded Lt. McCarthy. "Not a bad idea. Maybe he'll tell Leah why he needs so many sheets. Go on up, Leah."

Leah smiled and winked at her father. She was eager to speak to Mr. Brenner. "Room 503, on the fifth floor," Rabbi Lamdan said as she turned to go. "We'll meet you in a few minutes," he added cheerfully.

Leah walked over to the elevators. A large number of people were standing and waiting. She looked at her watch and frowned. "Should I walk up five flights?" she wondered to herself. She squinted at a stairway door and then decided to walk. After all, she considered, when she visited the hospital on Shabbos, she always walked up the stairs. She walked over to the stairway door and stepped inside. It was well lit as she moved toward the first landing.

After she had walked up the first flight of steps, she heard the door slam below. Someone else was taking the stairs. She looked over the banister and saw a doctor dressed in surgical green begin to walk up the steps. She particularly noticed his reddish-blond hair. She smiled to herself because from her vantage point above him it looked as if he had teased the front of his hair into a wave. Suddenly he looked up and saw her.

Leah moved uneasily up the stairs, quickening her pace. She was already on the second landing and he was almost behind her, so she began to move even faster. At the third floor she left the stairwell and entered the third-floor hallway. Leah heaved a sigh. *Since when had she become such a scaredy-cat!* she thought. She couldn't think of a reason for being so frightened. After all, he was a doctor here in the hospital! He had simply been taking the stairs, just as she had.

After a few minutes, she giggled to herself in embarrassment and returned to the stairwell to continue slowly up the stairs. On the fifth floor she stopped for a moment to catch her breath, and then entered the fifth-floor corridor. She saw the nurse at the station at the end of the corridor and turned to walk in that direction. She followed the numbers on the wall and stopped in front of Room 503.

Leah was eager to speak to Mr. Brenner, so she knocked on the door, waited a few seconds, and then stepped inside. Mr. Brenner was lying in bed and looking around nervously. "Nurse," he said weakly as Leah walked into the room and then said, with a relieved laugh, "Oh, it's you. Are you here with your father?"

Leah smiled back. "My father is downstairs. He'll be up in a few minutes," she explained. "What happened to your nephew? Why didn't he get your message?" she probed gently.

"That's a good question. But I can't answer it. Worse yet, my key didn't work," he snapped, unable to keep the hostility from his voice. "He must have changed the lock since I was last here — unless I was so cold that my fingers just couldn't fit the key into the lock. I waited for him to come home but I guess I waited longer than I should have, for I woke up here. Do you know when they'll let me out?"

Leah managed a wry smile. "Have you spoken to your nephew? When you leave the hospital, where will you go?" she asked.

Mr. Brenner shook his head grimly. He was nervous. "Do me a favor, I beg of you," he stammered in exhaustion. “Under a flap inside my jacket pocket I have my address book. Look under the name *Ari Brenner*. Call him for me. The phone by my night table doesn’t work and I have no cell phone.”

Leah stared at him in surprise. “He still hasn’t been reached?” she asked as she found Mr. Brenner’s jacket in the tiny closet and checked the pockets. There was a pocket-sized brown Tehillim with a Magen David on the cover. The lining under that revealed a small thin phone book. It was quite dog-eared.

“I use my phone book a lot,” he sighed mournfully. Mr. Brenner shifted in his bed and rubbed his eyes.

“I’ll be back soon,” Leah said as she walked back into the corridor. The telephones were at the end of the hall. Leah had no cell phone with her but she did have some coins, so she removed a coin from her purse and dialed the number. The phone rang at the other end. No one answered. She hung up and tried again. Again, there was no answer. Then she saw a listing for a phone number in Boston. The name next to it was *Chananya Brenner*, and next to that name, *Moshe Katz* appeared in parentheses. Leah shook her head sadly and stared into space.

Boston! That would be a long-distance call! Wouldn’t his son in Boston try to reach the nephew in New York? Wouldn’t Chananya be worried? Just then, as she looked back down the hall toward Mr. Brenner’s room, she saw the doctor with the reddish-blond hair and the wave on his forehead. He was pushing a patient seated in a wheelchair. The patient’s head was hanging down as the doctor in his operating-room greens carefully pulled the wheelchair out of the room and then turned the chair and moved away from Leah. Leah watched him make his way toward an exit. He seemed in a terrible hurry.

She gnawed her bottom lip and hesitated. Then she frowned and shrugged and dialed again. There was still no answer. "Oh, where are you?" she asked as calmly as she could manage. But then, Mr. Brenner's little phone book slipped out of her hands to the floor. She retrieved it and opened it to turn back to the page with Ari Brenner's number. She let out a sigh as she looked at the first page. The words "Aleph 02" were printed on the top of the page with a list of numbers: 12/16, 1/14, 2/13, 3/14, 4/12, 5/12, 6/10, 7/10, 8/09, 9/07, 10/07, 11/06, 12/05.

Leah froze. A vague fear descended upon her. What did these numbers mean? There were twelve in all and they looked like monthly dates for the year 2002. She fumbled through her purse, looking for a calendar for that year, but she could not find one. She shook her head again and forced herself to ignore her discomfiture.

Leah Lamdan, she said to herself, *What an overactive imagination you have!* Leah turned toward the telephone and dialed Ari Brenner's number. When the coin returned a third time, she heard the voices of her father and Lieutenant McCarthy. They seemed surprised and angry as they walked from the elevator to the nurses' station. Leah waved. Rabbi Lamdan saw her. She put the telephone back on its hook and pointed in the direction of Mr. Brenner's room. Rabbi Lamdan walked over to his daughter.

"Well," he sighed, "we now have a real mystery."

Leah waited. "Mr. Brenner has eight talleisim and a cache of silver coins," he said unexpectedly.

"So?" Leah queried. "Is it a crime to have many talleisim? Is it against the law to have many silver coins?"

Rabbi Lamdan nodded, frowning. "Actually, it may be. There has been a rash of robberies of silver coins. They were stolen from dealers who specialize in coins and medals. These coins were sewn like trinkets around the edges of the talleisim. The lieutenant suspects that some of these coins are the missing ones. He will have to take them and check them out with a numismatist," he said reluctantly.

Leah was dismayed. "Mr. Brenner doesn't look like a thief," she said.

"How does a thief look?" asked Lieutenant McCarthy as he approached them glumly. "I never heard of a 'look' called *thief*. You'd be surprised at how innocent many thieves 'look.'"

The three of them walked together toward Room 503. They opened the door and froze. It was an eerie feeling, and Leah felt it. After all, she had been in the room with Shimon Brenner a few moments earlier. Now the room was empty. Shimon Brenner was gone! He seemed to have disappeared! McCarthy summoned a nurse. No one had seen the patient leave. He could not have walked out of the hospital himself. Someone must have helped him!

Leah heaved a deep sigh. She remembered the doctor with the reddish-blond hair pushing a patient in a wheel chair. Perhaps he had seen Mr. Brenner leave? They walked over to the main desk on the floor. The lieutenant flashed his badge and asked to speak to the head nurse. His questions brought negative answers.

"We have no doctor on staff with reddish-blond hair," she said in a singsong voice. A haughty smile passed her lips. "I'm quite familiar with all the staff members who are authorized to work on this floor."

McCarthy seemed to bristle with indignation. He looked toward Leah and frowned. Then he turned back to the head nurse. "You may know your staff," he gritted through his teeth, "but you *don't* know the whereabouts of your patients."

The head nurse blushed a deep red. She shrugged and turned away from McCarthy. "Kidnapping is your business, not ours," she said as she walked into her private office.

Leah was disheartened. "I feel foolish," she said. "I must have seen the kidnapper in action and I didn't realize it. The more I think about it, the more I believe that the kidnapper was the man with the reddish-blond hair. He must have wheeled Mr. Brenner out of here."

"Don't worry," said the lieutenant. "We'll find them. We'll find them both!"

After a few more minutes, Rabbi Lamdan offered to drive Leah to school. She walked to the car with him, feeling very unhappy.

"Don't worry about it," assured her father. "I am sure that there is a simple explanation for all of this. There's a reason we met Mr. Brenner; there's a reason he froze outside his nephew's apartment, and there is a reason he has disappeared. Sometimes it just takes time to find out why."

Myriad thoughts swirled around in Leah's mind. It was really too depressing, She wanted to get to school and talk to her friends. As her father braked the car in front of the school building, a student came outside and happily waved to the car.

"No school!" she shouted. "The boiler broke down! No school today!"

Leah rolled down her window. She stared straight at the girl. "No school," she repeated.

"We made a chain call but you weren't home. We have the day off." Leah looked back at her father as the girl walked away. She lived only a few blocks from

Bais Malkah High and didn't need a ride. Rabbi Lamdan observed his daughter.

"I'll drive you home," he said. "I am sure that your mother and aunt will find plenty for you to do."

But Leah's thoughts were still on Mr. Brenner, so she just nodded her head and accepted the ride home. As he dropped her off in front of the house, he said softly to her. "Don't forget that today is Rosh Chodesh. You must say Hallel and Mussaf when you daven."

Leah nodded and closed her eyes tiredly. When she opened them again, her lips began to quiver. "I will say Tehillim also," she said.

Rabbi Lamdan tried to soothe her, to no avail. Shaking his head, he started the motor again. "I'm late!" he remarked as he looked at his watch. It was 9 o'clock. "Can you imagine that all this has happened to us already and it's still only 9 o'clock in the morning?" He looked again at Leah and smiled. "Often a chain of events makes no sense to us. For example, Avraham Avinu was told by Hashem that his children would be enslaved in a foreign land. He did not know which land would oppress them. He did not know how his children would get to that land. Would they be free men or slaves?

"Because of the story of Yosef and his brothers, Yaakov Avinu left Canaan and traveled to Egypt. Thus, the children of Avraham and Yaakov came to Egypt as free men. The jealousy of the brothers of Yosef was the means leading to Israel's sojourn in Egypt and the fulfillment of Hashem's prophecy to Avraham.

"Hashem works in miraculous ways. That is why we make a berachah, even when we hear bad news. We say, 'Baruch Dayan HaEmes.' Sometimes something bad leads to something good.

"We must do what we can but we must always daven to Hashem. Take care of your mother and aunt. I hope, with the help of Hashem, to be home for lunch."

She left the car as he waved his hand and then drove off. Once in the house, Leah was surprised to find her mother sitting comfortably in front of a wireless laptop computer.

"My sister arranged for this computer to be delivered to our house by 8 o'clock this morning. Can you imagine that?"

After Leah finished davening, her mother explained to her, "I am using it like a word processor. It's really a very exciting experience. I'm typing the minutes of previous N'shei meetings. Do you know that this computer corrects spelling mistakes, sets margins, and eliminates errors? It's fantastic! I'm very impressed."

Leah smiled back at her mother. "But how is your leg?" she asked

"It does bother me a little," was the reply. "It's not easy to find a comfortable position to sit in when you're wearing a cast, but I enjoy the computer enough that it takes away my feelings of discomfort."

Leah smiled broadly. "You're coming of age," she giggled.

"Do you think knowing how to use the computer makes me younger? Nonsense, Leah! I am merely amazed at what a computer can do."

Leah brightened. "Dodah Devorah got you hooked in less than an hour!" she exclaimed.

"That's true," admitted Mrs. Lamdan. She laughed and raised one eyebrow. "The word processor is just like typing, and typing was a required elective when I went to school. Can you imagine such a phrase? It was a *required* elective?"

Leah laughed again. Mothers could sometimes say strange things! She knew that her mother and Dodah Devorah had been up half the night together, talking about all sorts of things. She had expected both of them to sleep late that morning, yet here they were, already at work!

"Where *is* Dodah Devorah?" she blurted out.

Her mother drew a long breath, exhaled, and then smiled. "My sister is on the phone. Something was missing from my computer so she wanted to call a store and get the missing part. I think that she plans to go to Manhattan today to pick it up."

Just then Dodah Devorah emerged from the kitchen, carrying a small plastic envelope tucked under one arm and a blue pen in the other hand.

"Where can I get a car?' she asked.

"Do you want me to call a car service for you?" asked Leah as she reached for the telephone directory.

"I must go to 47th Street in Manhattan. Is that the 'Diamond Center'?" She squinted and hesitated, then leaned forward to pay closer attention. Her brow furrowed and she closed her eyes for a moment. She turned and looked at her sister with deep intensity.

Mrs. Lamdan looked up from the computer and smiled. She liked to keep an immaculate house, as it made her feel organized and in control. The fact that she was now immobilized had made her both uncomfortable and unhappy. She had been upset because she was unable to do the things that she wanted to do and go to the places where she wanted to go. She hadn't felt like herself at all. Then her sister had come and opened a door to many interesting activities. Suddenly she found herself busy with so many new things to do and so many new ways to do them. The computer was exciting! But, still, there were many things that had to be done and could not be done by just sitting in front of a monitor.

"You know," she said to her sister, "if you're planning on going to Manhattan to the jewelry center, I have a favor to ask of you. I broke an earring while I was taking it off last week. Perhaps you can take it to a jeweler for me and it can be fixed while you wait."

"Of course, I can. Please tell me anything else I can do to help you," replied Dodah Devorah. "After all, I came to help."

"Maybe Leah can go with you. I think that she would enjoy spending time with you, especially in Manhattan. Leah rarely gets a day off from school, and when she does, I don't have the time to take her to the city. So," she grinned hopefully, "how about the two of you spending the day together?"

"I don't think that we should leave you here in the house, all by yourself," Dodah Devorah replied and lowered her voice. "What happens if someone rings the doorbell? How can you get around?"

Mrs. Lamdan pooh-poohed Devorah's concerns. "I'll pretend that Leah is in school. It's not the first time that I've been alone ... and it's only for a short period of time."

Leah gave her mother a cautious look. She put her finger on her lips. "I think Dodah Devorah may be right."

"No!" her mother shook her head. "I would appreciate it very much if the two of you would go to Manhattan. I can talk to myself while I type and not feel so inhibited."

Dodah Devorah laughed. "I remember that you always typed out loud."

"Please don't give away all my secrets," Leah's mother said with a smile.

Leah called a local car service that arrived in front of the house in just a few minutes. En route, Dodah Devorah did not talk much. She silently watched the highways pulsating with colorful cars that passed them like flagships on parade. Her eyes glowed with satisfaction as the car moved quietly toward the Brooklyn Bridge. Leah, sitting next to her aunt in the back seat, also enjoyed the trip to Manhattan. She loved the New York skyline, with its big buildings jutting upward like sandcastles on the beach. She also enjoyed sitting next to her aunt and observing her face as she quietly observed the vibrancy of New York City.

Dodah Devorah smiled. Leah loved her smile. In the beginning it was like a trickle of a smile and suddenly it would explode in laughter. Leah gazed at her aunt. She was trim and elegant. The lines on her face signified character and laughter. How could that be for a woman who had suffered so much? But the serenity was there. It was a radiant serenity. Leah remembered a remark her aunt had once made after arranging a tzedakah clothing drive for a yeshivah and donating time and money toward it.

"It is one of the beautiful compensations of life that by helping another we can help ourselves."

CHAPTER 3

DODAH DEVORAH

Devorah Goodwin was a 35-year-old widow who had become a professional international consultant in the past two-and-a-half years. Before that she had helped her husband at home with the unending legal work in his office. They had had two children, both of whom had died from the dreaded Tay-Sachs disease, five and six years earlier. Almost three years after those tragedies, her husband had been killed in a terrorist attack at the synagogue they attended when in Paris. It was Yom Tov and he had been called up to the Torah. As he made his way toward the bimah, three Arab terrorists pulled out their rifles and began shooting. Hersh Goodwin had just begun to raise his tallis over his head when they shot him.

From the women's section, Devorah saw her husband fall. She quickly moved aside the curtain and ran over to him. He died in her arms, his tallis red with blood, the stains lining the collar where the new silver atarah was to have been attached. Rabbi and Mrs. Lamdan had rushed to Paris to be near Devorah during the shivah and to plead with her to move to New York and live with them.

"Life must go on. You have experienced so many nisyonos; we don't know why. But an even greater tragedy would occur if you allowed anguish and despair to rule over you."

Dodah Devorah had refused even to consider resettling in America. And all the time she mourned, she clutched the new atarah for her husband's tallis that she had planned to sew on for that Shabbos but had forgotten to. That was the reason he had not been wearing it with his new tallis. Now, more than two years later, the silver atarah looked tarnished, somewhat crimson. It had become the brownish-purple of silver as it oxidizes.

Rabbi Lamdan returned to the United States from France before his wife, as he had to resume teaching at the yeshivah where he was a rebbi. He told Leah that she would temporarily share her room with her aunt. Leah agreed, although it tore at her heart to think of the kind of sorrow that had struck Dodah Devorah. What would she be like now? Dodah Devorah had always laughed so much! Would she ever laugh again?

However, Dodah Devorah had refused to come at that time, and Leah did not have to share her room. Two weeks later, Mrs. Lamdan had returned home without her sister. Dodah Devorah announced that she would create a memorial for her husband and sons; nothing would deter her. She contacted her husband's friends who had contacts with other lawyers and many different companies and introduced herself as a proficient and experienced editor in the English language. Did anyone have correspondence to be translated? She could write summaries and resumés in English, French, Yiddish, and Hebrew.

Devorah Goodwin had a working knowledge of Russian because of her dealings with that new immigrant population. She had also begun to study Arabic and Chinese. She grasped languages easily, and international companies hired her as a consultant to review all written material. She was a translator *par excellence*, and many different groups and organizations sought her advice on the wording of various contracts and deals. During those two-and-a-half years, Devorah Goodwin Inc. had become a multinational consulting company. She earned a great deal of money and set up special scholarship funds in various yeshivahs in London, Paris, and Israel — all in memory of her dear husband and two sons. But the work and constant business activities were excessive. Sometimes it seemed as if she worked all 24 hours of the day. She was not happy with her situation, and a friend suggested that she "take a break." Yes, she agreed. She needed a break ... and then her sister in America broke her leg!

The driver stopped at 47th Street and 6th Avenue. Dodah Devorah suddenly enveloped Leah with her warm, soft smile and tilted her head to the right.

"Let's go," she urged. Then she turned to the driver: "G-d willing, we'll be back in an hour."

The driver tipped his hat. "I may leave for a short while if the police tell me to move the car, or I may want to run the motor by driving around for a short while. But don't worry if you come out and I'm not here — I'll be back."

As they got out of the car Leah turned to her aunt. "Have you ever been to the Jewelry Exchange?"

"Hersh used to come here every year. He usually bought me presents when he returned from the States. Either he had very good taste in jewelry or he knew a salesman who had excellent taste, because the pieces were always lovely."

"Did he buy you birthday presents?"

"We didn't celebrate birthdays, but every Rosh Chodesh Shevat, Hersh brought me something."

"Isn't that your Hebrew birthday month?"

"Yes," she nodded. "Hersh believed in celebrating special Hebrew dates. To us, Rosh Chodesh, the first day of the new month, was always a time for celebration. Do you know, Leah, that the Rosh Chodesh of every month is a Jewish holiday for women?"

Leah chuckled. "Of course, I know," she said. She loved to repeat what she had learned, and went on. "When Bnei Yisrael were in the wilderness and Moshe Rabbeinu went up on Har Sinai to receive the Torah, the Jews became afraid that Moshe would not return to them. They ordered Moshe's brother, Aharon, to create a god designed for them. As a delay tactic, Aharon told the people to gather all their gold jewelry and said that he would melt it down to create an idol for them. The men willingly donated their rings and their other gold jewelry. The women, however, refused to comply. After all the miracles of the Exodus, the women believed that Hashem would not let them down. They believed that Moshe would return. Meanwhile, Aharon took the men's gold jewelry and melted it down. A golden calf arose from the ashes. When Moshe came down from the mountain, and saw the people dancing around the golden calf and bowing before it, he threw down the Luchos inscribed with the words of the Ten Commandments and broke them.

Afterwards, he went up on Har Sinai again to receive the second set of Luchos.

"Because the women refused to give their jewelry for the creation of the golden calf, Hashem granted them a special holiday, Rosh Chodesh, the first day of every Hebrew month. Thus, women are recognized and praised on the first day of every month of the Jewish calendar for our devotion to and love for Hashem."

Dodah Devorah smiled. For a moment she leaned against the doorjamb, staring into space. "Thanks, Leah. It's good to be with you again. I forgot how much you love to repeat the divrei Torah you have learned!"

Leah followed her aunt into the electronics store. In minutes they had completed their transaction and Dodah Devorah's package was in her hands. They stepped out into the cold air. "I'll return this to the car so I won't have to carry it as we walk around," she said to Leah. "Wait here." But Dodah Devorah returned in less than a minute. The driver had already left. "At least it isn't a big package," she smiled.

"I'll gladly carry it for you," offered Leah.

Dodah Devorah shook her head and Leah followed her into the Diamond Exchange. Leah took her mother's earring from her pocket. She spotted Mr. Kaufman's counter and walked over to his section. The Lamdans knew the Kaufman family from their Kensington neighborhood, and the Kaufmans' son and Leah's brother Moshe were in the same class in the yeshivah. Leah handed Mr. Kaufman the earring and showed him the piece that had broken off.

"I can't fix it today," he said. "I may have it ready tomorrow. If you wish, I'll give it to your father in shul so that you won't have to come back to Manhattan. I heard that the Bais Malkah School's boiler broke down, and that it will probably be fixed by this afternoon. So you won't have another day off tomorrow!" he said, laughing.

Dodah Devorah had walked over to a different counter. She was pointing to an item in a glass case and discussing something with the owner. Leah walked over to see what had interested her aunt. "That atarah," she pointed out a gleaming object, "it's like the atarah I bought for Hersh. And I thought Hersh's atarah was one-of-a-kind," she mused. She stared into the distance for a moment and then sighed.

"All atarahs look alike to me," said Leah.

"This one was different," explained her aunt. "Most atarahs have small squares of silver attached to each other to make a panel that is sewn onto the tallis. Mine, or rather Hersh's, was of round pieces, like this one, but this atarah seems to be much thicker than the one that I purchased in London."

"The atarah is for the tallis," reminded Leah. "Are you considering buying another atarah? Is something going on that my mother doesn't know about?" Leah's eyes twinkled with delight at her not-so-subtle hint, but Dodah Devorah looked embarrassed.

"No," she said after a few seconds. "Nothing is 'going on.' It's just that the atarah reminded me of ..." She stopped in mid-sentence and Leah was sure she saw a tear beginning to seep from the corner of her aunt's right eye. Dodah Devorah took a deep breath as she turned toward another counter. She rubbed her eyes and blinked. "I remember when I was 8 years old, my mother registered me for a sewing class. I wanted to design a beautiful cloak with a high stand-up collar surrounding the neck like a crown. I described the details to my teacher and told her that I planned on making a royal purple and white design with sequins of silver on the collar. My teacher laughed and asked me if I got the design from the "Tallis Weaver of Iran." Then she told the class this story that she had read in a book, *Secret Weapons of the Jews*. This story was from Baghdad.

"There was once a poor man who made talleisim. He was quite skillful and his talleisim were beautiful. He was a very religious man and constantly prayed to Hashem to help him earn a better living. The tallis weaver had only one daughter and he wanted her to marry a true talmid chacham, but he wondered how he could ever afford a dowry worthy of such a man. His dream was to weave the most beautiful tallis for his future son-in-law, and the tallis itself would extol the character of the wearer.

"One Friday night, the tallis weaver stayed late in shul to say a few extra chapters of Tehillim for his daughter's benefit. He saw a stranger sitting alone in the back of the shul, so he approached him and invited him to his Shabbos table.

"The stranger said beautiful divrei Torah at the Shabbos table and the tallis weaver was entranced by what he said. After the meal, when everyone else had gone to sleep, the two walked outside to continue talking. Suddenly the stranger grabbed the tallis weaver, lifted him up, and flew with him toward Heaven. The tallis weaver was frightened and closed his eyes.

"'Look at the tapestry of the world!' said the stranger. The tallis weaver opened his eyes and saw a tallis of exquisite beauty stretched across the earth. The reflection of the stars twinkling and dancing were the crown of this beautiful tallis. The tallis weaver gaped in awe and said a berachah thanking Hashem for letting him see such a view. When he returned home and the guest had gone on his way, the tallis weaver told his wife about the beautiful tallis in the sky.

"She stared at him and shook her head sadly. She wondered, *How will our daughter ever get married? My dear husband is losing his mind! No one will want to marry into our family if it were known that the girl's father sees strange guests!*

"'We had no Shabbos guest," she berated him after he had repeated the story many times.

"He turned to his daughter but she agreed with her mother. 'Father,' she said quietly, 'we had no Shabbos guest this past Shabbos day.'

"Two days later the Shah of Iran announced his daughter's betrothal. With joy in his heart he unlocked a special cedar closet to remove the precious veil to be worn by the princess on her wedding day. This was a unique veil that had been handed down for generations. But to his dismay, the veil was moth-eaten and had become ragged and torn. The Shah summoned his advisers and weavers. All were afraid to handle such delicate threads.

"Our tallis weaver was brought to the Shah's palace, too. When he saw the veil he recognized its intricate design, for it was similar to the Earth-tallis he had seen. 'With Hashem's guidance and help, I will try,' he offered.

"Two months later, he had succeeded in restoring the beautiful veil to the Shah. In appreciation the Shah presented him with a chest of gold and silver. The tallis weaver gave almost everything in the chest to the poor and needy Jews of Iran, holding back only the amount he needed to 'create' a tallis for his future son-in-law.

"Need I tell you, within the year, his daughter married a prominent talmid chacham whose beautiful tallis was merely a cover for his good nature, his favorable character traits, and his ability to learn Torah."

Dodah Devorah touched Leah gently on the cheek. "I have a beautiful atarah," she said, "but it needs someone to wear it. It is almost like having a mezuzah case of silver without the parchment inside. I still hope that one day I will polish the atarah and see it being used as it should be. That's why I can't sell it."

"I'm sorry," mumbled Leah sadly, "I didn't mean ...."

But Dodah Devorah shook her head. "It's not you," she said. "It's life, and there are so many things in life we have to get used to." She took a tissue from her purse and blew her nose. She looked up again and smiled at her niece. Then she pointed to a door marked "Women" and began walking toward it.

"I must powder my nose," she said. "Wait here for me." Leah nodded and turned her attention toward a different counter.

Chapter 4

Suspect at Large

That was when she saw him! She became suddenly alert. He was tall, sleek, and slightly overdressed. The shoulders of his jacket were too padded and the lapel too pointed. But it was his hair that she remembered. It was thick, reddish-blond, and curly, with a wave over his forehead. A hardly noticeable pencil-thin mustache traced his upper lip. He was talking — no — arguing with someone at the counter. He smiled a mechanical smile, polite but neither warm nor cordial. Then he looked around the large Exchange at the many different jewelry counters. His fingers played with something in his hand, and, as he put a square pad down on the counter, he nodded and began to walk toward the door. From the distance of three counters across the way, Leah recognized the small

It was a pocket-size Tehillim with a Magen David on the cover. Leah looked nervously toward the door marked "Women," and then her eyes followed the man with the reddish-blond hair as he opened the Exchange door. He was leaving! She looked at the man behind the counter where she was standing, and, after hesitating for a moment, began to speak rapidly to him.

"My aunt is in the ladies' room. She'll be out in a second and I just remembered something I must do outside. Please tell her that I will meet her by the car, G-d willing. I must hurry now ..." and then she headed rapidly toward the door.

Outside, she saw the man with the reddish-blond hair crossing the street in the middle of the block. She pulled out a small pad and pencil she always carried in her pocket and began to write down things that she noticed about him and that she wanted to remember. He walked to Sixth Avenue, turned right, and kept on walking. Leah began to follow him hesitantly. Then she saw the driver who had brought them to Manhattan. He was standing in front of his car, reading a newspaper. He looked up and saw Leah. He waved to her and Leah waved back. Then she made a hasty decision to follow the man with the reddish-blond hair!

He turned around once and looked behind him as if suddenly suspecting that he was being followed. At that moment, Leah pulled the collar of her winter jacket up to cover her cheeks and maybe even hide her face somewhat to avoid the possibility of being recognized. Then she looked at her watch. She felt that she still had to follow him; she wanted to know where he was going. The man strode to another block, this time not looking back at all. He passed an open door near a dress shop and then walked in the direction of a very tall building.

He entered the marble lobby. Leah stopped for a moment, working up her courage and observing him through the huge glass doors. He was studying the floor directory. Then he marched determinedly into one of the elevators. Leah watched him go inside and as the door to the elevator closed, she hurried inside, looked up, and watched the pointer to see on which floor the elevator would stop. The elevator ascended to the seventh floor and stopped.

The guard near the entrance broke into her thoughts. "What's your business, young lady? Whom do you want to see?" the guard said roughly. He leaned forward and shot her an angry glance. He clearly did not allow anyone to loiter in the building.

"What business is on the seventh floor?" she asked impulsively. It really wasn't like her to be so intrusive. Leah's knees were quaking. She didn't remember ever having done anything like this before. The guard looked at her oddly, studying her. He cleared his throat.

"The seventh floor? You are asking about a business on the seventh floor? Who are you? Why is it *your* business?" he asked gruffly.

She backed away from him and shrugged her shoulders. Then she mumbled an apology and left the building. Once outside she looked at her watch again. She quickly wrote down the building's address and ran back to the car service. Dodah Devorah was already there.

"Nice timing," she said. "Where were you? The man behind the jewelry counter told me that you ran out of the store because you forgot something. I couldn't think of anything you might have forgotten. I have the package from the electronics store and you gave Mr. Kaufman your mother's earring. So tell me, Leah, where did you go?" she said sternly.

"I'm sorry, Dodah Devorah, I thought I saw someone I knew."

"That's not a reason to disappear." Dodah Devorah's voice was tense. "I, too, saw someone I recognized. I went back to the man behind the counter where I saw the beautiful atarah I liked. The sales clerk was talking to a gentleman whose face looked familiar.

"'Mr. Kaufman, Mr. Kaufman,' he called out loudly. 'Our man left. He's disappeared!'

"But it wasn't your Mr. Kaufman to whom you gave your mother's earring. It was my Mr. Klein! I recognized him immediately. It was the gentleman who did not have enough cash for a first-class ticket.

"I was stunned. I was positive that he had told me his name was Mr. Klein, yet this jeweler was calling him Mr. Kaufman. I cleared my throat and said hesitantly, 'Mr. Klein, are you the Mr. Klein I met at the airport?'

"He looked startled, as well he should. I guess my face registered surprise, but so did his.

"'Hello,' he said to me in a friendly tone. But I saw that he looked worried. He looked at a man behind one of the counters and then looked back at me. 'Is your sister feeling better?' he asked me.

"I began to stutter an answer but he excused himself and ran out. The young man who had summoned him was quite anxious, too."

Leah frowned. She was listening to her aunt, yet her mind was also concentrating on something else. "So where did Mr. Kaufman, also known as Mr. Klein, go?" she asked.

"I don't know. What I do know is that he introduced himself to me as Mr. Klein. Of that I am now quite certain." Dodah Devorah paused to let her words sink in. "I know, because I wrote down the information he gave me about himself in my traveling diary when I initially handed him the money. See?"

Leah listened in breathless silence. As she read the information in Dodah Devorah's diary, her mind was also busy with thoughts about the man with the reddish-blond hair. "Please," Leah pleaded with her aunt, "can you wait for a few minutes? I must make a phone call."

"I don't mind in the least," said her aunt. "But first tell me: Are you on some mystery case?"

Leah nodded. With a twinkle in her eye, her aunt opened her purse, took out a cell phone, and handed it to Leah. Suddenly Leah was startled to see the man with the reddish-blond hair emerge from a building across the street. He began to stride up and down in front of a store window, mumbling angrily to himself.

Dodah Devorah saw the look on Leah's face. "Is that our mystery man?" she asked.

"Yes," replied Leah thoughtfully. Suddenly, a large black car drew near the intersection and blocked them from seeing the man. Someone inside the car waved to him. Leah furrowed her brow. Were her suspicions correct? Was this man with the reddish-blond hair the same man she had seen dressed as a doctor in the hospital? Could she be mistaken? Shouldn't she first go back to the counter where she had seen him place the Tehillim and verify that this was the Tehillim that belonged to Mr. Brenner? Was she getting ahead of herself? Maybe there was no mystery at all! The man with the reddish-blond hair got into the black car.

"Follow that car!" Dodah Devorah ordered her driver. The car-service driver revved his engine, leaned back in his seat, buckled his seat belt, and turned to Dodah Devorah.

"This may cost you much more money," he said. "Are you sure that you don't want to just call the police?"

Dodah Devorah shook her head stubbornly. He started the car moving. The black car turned toward Tenth Avenue.

Leah tried to sound casual. "I think that we are going in the direction of home," she said. They were four car lengths behind the black car as it took the West Side Highway to the Brooklyn Battery Tunnel.

"They're going to Brooklyn!" exulted Dodah Devorah, "and so are we!" The black car stopped near the outskirts of Borough Park. Its passenger got out and stood for a moment in front of a brownstone building. The man with the reddish-blond hair waved goodbye to his driver and entered the building. Leah wrote down the address as their driver took them back to her house.

Chapter 5

Disappearing Coins

Her mother was drinking hot tea, still sitting in front of the computer and smiling. Dodah Devorah dropped the package from the electronics store onto the couch and opened it. She walked over to the computer and began to study it. Then she looked back at her sister and nodded. Her face looked serious and anxious.

"Leah told me that the Mr. Brenner we picked up from the airport yesterday has disappeared."

Mrs. Lamdan eased back into the cushioned chair at the desk and sighed. "Worse yet, the police suspect that Mr. Brenner is involved in the theft of silver coins from the International Kaspi Silver Medals Organization. It looks like some of these coins come from Europe and were smuggled into our country. Interpol — the International Police — are now also checking into other recent robberies involving coins," she said.

Dodah Devorah looked grim. Suddenly her face brightened. "I've helped Interpol twice before, "she said, smiling slyly. " One of the cases that I was involved in concerned computer hackers. I learned some interesting things about police computers while I helped them access different codes to catch the thieves. I still have a few contacts in Interpol in case some emergency comes up."

Mrs. Lamdan stared wide-eyed at her sister. "Can you find out if the coins Mr. Brenner had were stolen? He's from Boston, not from Europe."

Dodah Devorah frowned. "The police found Mr. Brenner's passport. He is an international traveler, and he really travels a great deal. People who are involved in all kinds of nefarious activities often try to involve innocent wayfarers in their schemes."

Leah pushed a chair closer to the computer and sat down. "What do you propose to do?" she asked.

Dodah Devorah smiled tentatively. "What I'll do is contact my friends at Interpol and ask them to run the information we have through their database of criminals." She settled down at the computer and began to press various keys on the keyboard. Leah watched in fascination. Within five minutes Dodah Devorah had a computer printout. "They can cross-check this list of recent silver coin thefts," she announced, "and find out if any of the suspects in these thefts match the features of your reddish-blond man or perhaps the features of Mr. Brenner."

Someone rang the doorbell. Leah stood up to answer the door. It was Lieutenant McCarthy. Leah was glad to see him, noting that the lieutenant was not alone.

"Mrs. Lamdan, Mrs. Goodwin, and Leah Lamdan," Lieutenant McCarthy introduced them to the young man standing beside him. "Meet Moshe Katz from Boston!"

Moshe Katz's smile was polite as his gaze traveled around the room and settled on Mrs. Lamdan. He noted that her leg was in a cast. "I'm sorry to disturb you," he began. "I don't understand why the lieutenant found it necessary to bring me here at all. I am looking for Mr. Shimon Brenner. Is he here? Do you know where he is?"

Leah, who had returned to her place near the computer, now turned to study the young man. Speculatively, she tilted her head to one side and watched as Dodah Devorah answered his question.

"We've met Mr. Brenner," she explained. "We're the ones who took him from the airport to Borough Park."

His reaction was fiercely defensive. Leah could see that even before he spoke. "I didn't get his message until late. I tried to contact his nephew but there was no answer."

McCarthy saw that Katz's explanation was lacking, and flashed a smile as he obligingly filled in the blanks. "Moshe Katz is the caregiver for Chanaya Brenner, who lives in Boston. Mr. Katz was hired about eight months ago by Mr. Shimon Brenner to care for Chanaya, who is a quadriplegic. Mr. Brenner hired Mr. Katz after a five-minute interview, because he was desperate to find a nurse for his son. Mr. Brenner travels a lot, you see, and he wanted to make sure that Chananya had good help."

Leah's mother coughed and cleared her throat. "I empathize with Mr. Katz and young Mr. Brenner. But the case can wait while we eat. Perhaps you would like to join us for lunch? In that way we can enjoy your company and learn a little more about Mr. Brenner."

Mr. Katz smiled good-naturedly and nodded. Then he turned to McCarthy. "Is that why you suggested that we come here? Do you want some information from me?"

McCarthy shifted his feet and sighed. His tone had turned very gentle. "We are all interested in sharing information to find out more about Mr. Brenner and his antics. Yours truly, as well."

Leah saw her mother signal Dodah Devorah that they should all move into the kitchen and sit down there. Her mother wore an oddly pinched expression. Moshe Katz looked around the room curiously and then sat down on a chair not far from a window. Leah smiled to herself as she studied him. *He looks nervous enough to want to jump out of the window,* she thought. Leah glanced at his expression, but decided that she really could not interpret the look that crossed his face. Abruptly he moved the chair closer to the table and rubbed the palms of his hands together nervously. When he spoke his voice was much more brisk than before. He looked as if he had felt a pang of guilt, and he took a couple of deep breaths before he began to speak.

"When I first met Mr. Brenner," he said, "he was anxious and worried about his son, Chananya. He told me that I was a godsend to him. He pays me minimum wage, but he also gives me room and board. So my basic needs are covered. My job is to be with Chananya, especially since his father cannot be with him all the time." He suddenly began to cough. Leah hurried to the sink and filled a glass with water. She brought it to him, then leaned over the countertop, lifted a box of tissues, and set that down on the table as well. She moved toward a chair in front of him and stared into his eyes.

"What do you do for Chananya?" she asked in a half-whisper, trying to encourage him to talk.

"Chananya and I share an apartment across the street from Boston Hospital. My job is to care for Chananya and listen to his doctors. They tell me when to bring Chananya to the hospital and I wait with him wherever he has to go. I am called a shadow and I guess you can understand why."

McCarthy gave him a cool assessing glance. "How often does Mr. Brenner get to see his son?" he asked, "and, since you are here today, who is with the young man today?"

"Chananya is in the hosital for some tests. As I told you at the hospital, Mr. Brenner left me a message to contact his nephew Ari. I tried to reach Ari but to no avail. And now, I cannot find Mr. Brenner. I'm worried about Mr. Brenner's health. He is not a well man and I know that he is very concerned about his son."

McCarthy shook his head knowingly. He turned to look at Leah's mother and aunt and then toward Leah. "My men met Mr. Katz at Mr. Brenner's nephew's place in Borough Park. When they told me about Mr. Katz and said that he was trying to find a Mr. Brenner, I decided to bring him here." He stopped abruptly and glanced down at his watch impatiently.

"How often does Mr. Brenner visit his son?" Leah repeated McCarthy's earlier question.

"Not often enough. Chananya misses his father very much, so no amount of time is ever enough. Mr. Brenner tries to come at least three times a week, but he can't stay long, as he must return to work." He breathed a long sigh.

Leah nodded and then continued to ask quietly. "What does Mr. Brenner do?"

Moshe Katz looked surprised at her question. "He's a jeweler, one of the best. He designs special pieces for important clients. But, as you probably know, the jewelry business is not very good today. No one is secure, not even a specialist like Mr. Brenner. He told me that he was very lucky to get another job as quickly as he did. He is paid well, but, his expenses are high. The bills for Chananya's care keep growing. We were lucky that we found each other."

Dodah Devorah leaned across the table, looking somewhat nervously at Moshe Katz' face. She shrugged and nodded at the same time while he continued to talk, for he suddenly began to look familiar. She told him this. "I feel that I know you."

Moshe Katz sighed. A hot flush suffused his face. "My family is from London," he said.

"*Do* I know you?" she raised an eyebrow.

"I don't think that I know you," he replied, "but perhaps you've heard of my family. We were originally from London but once — after much persuasion by my mother — our family went to Paris for Yom Tov. My mother was killed during a terrorist attack." He angled his head to one side. "That's why I left Europe about three years ago and have not been back. My father and siblings moved to Australia but I came here, to the United States."

Dodah Devorah had given an audible gasp during Katz's answer. Suddenly Leah was aware that her aunt's right hand was quivering. Casually Leah slid her hand into her aunt's and applied gentle pressure on the wrist until it stilled. The family immediately knew the cause of Devorah Goodkin's edginess and they saw the impact of Moshe Katz's words on her.

Lieutenant McCarthy shifted his weight in his chair and leaned forward on his elbows. "Why was Mr. Brenner carrying so many talleisim?" he asked.

Moshe Katz started, and then looked down, pink flooding his cheeks. "Talleisim? I was not aware that he had so many talleisim. I never saw him with more than one and, of course, his Tehillim. He always carries his Tehillim on his person."

Lieutenant McCarthy looked at Leah and shrugged. He steepled his fingers as he thought about the next question that he wanted to ask. His eyes locked on Leah, who turned and looked away. "How about the violin? Did you ever hear him play?"

Moshe Katz's face registered surprise. "Violin? I guess I really know very little about him." He shook his head in frustration. "I only know that he needed help for his son, and I needed help, too. At the time, the two of us seemed like a good match."

Mrs. Lamdan nodded her head and smiled back at him. "It's not an easy job you do. You must have a heart of gold! You're not only dealing with a sickly son but probably a very unhappy father. One of the qualities separating a two-legged person from a four-legged animal is compassion. We stand on two feet so that our arms are free to reach out and help someone," A half-smile crept across her face.

"I'm glad I can help Chananya," he said sadly, "but I came to New York today to speak to his father about something quite important. Where is Mr. Brenner?"

He looked around the room at the people there and shook his head glumly. Lieutenant McCarthy looked at Leah wordlessly. A tiny flurry of emotion passed across her face. She stared down at the table in front of her and then looked back at McCarthy.

"I'm not sure where Mr. Brenner is," she confessed hesitantly, "but I have two addresses that I would like the police to check out." McCarthy's eyes widened with surprise. A wide smile spread across his face.

"What kind of addresses? Where did you get them?"

Leah waited a few seconds before answering. She walked over to her winter jacket, which was hanging on a hook near the back door. She removed a piece of paper from the pocket. "That's a long story," she said. "First let me give you these addresses."

The computer suddenly began to beep, signaling that a message had been received. "What gives?" asked the lieutenant, twisting around to look closely at the computer. He looked at Dodah Devorah questioningly as she printed out the message.

She smiled. "I have helped Interpol often during the past two years, so I contacted my code advisers and told them what I was searching for. There have been many coin thefts lately in Europe and these 'missing' coins have been appearing here in the United States." Her voice dropped and it was not easy to hear her as she reached for the printout to study it.

In the meantime, Leah was beaming as she passed her slip of paper to the lieutenant. "I think I saw the man with the reddish-blond hair on 47th Street in the city today. He went to this address, to the seventh floor of this address," and she read the address aloud.

Dodah Devorah gasped. She ran to the coat closet and opened the door hastily. "I know that address," she said. "I am sure that that is the address I was given." She found her coat and slipped her hand into her pocket. A smile curled on her lips as she displayed a card in her palm. She stared at the card and frowned. "The plot thickens," she joked in a mysterious tone of voice as she read aloud the address on the card and the name of the man who gave her the card. "Mr. S. Bishop," she repeated as she closed her eyes and shuddered. "He deals with Jewish artifacts. But what does he have to do with Mr. Brenner?"

Dodah Devorah was not smiling. Just then, someone rang the doorbell. They heard quick footsteps and Rabbi Lamdan stepped into the kitchen. "Hello!" he said cheerfully. "Is everything all right? You look like you've seen a ghost!"

Mrs. Lamdan's face brightened at the sight of her husband. She had confidence that the mystery would be successfully resolved now that he had joined them. "Lunchtime!" she announced. "The best time to hash things over is while you're eating. During a meal all our juices flow and the brain works best when the body is satisfied.

"Won't you all join us?" she asked Moshe Katz and the lieutenant. "We will start with a bowl of hot soup and then a kugel — a pudding — that my sister made especially for Rosh Chodesh, the beginning of the new month."

Moshe Katz smiled. "Thank you," he said. "This will be an unexpected pleasure. My mother, too, used to make a special treat every Rosh Chodesh. Rosh Chodesh is a holiday for women and my mother would take pleasure in celebrating it by making something special that we all liked."

"Well, it's not a holiday for me!" said the lieutenant. "I want to check out this address now. The whole case is getting to be more and more mysterious. I'm anxious to move things along."

Rabbi Lamdan accompanied Lieutenant McCarthy to the door, and when he returned to the kitchen he asked his wife, "Has Mr. Brenner been found yet?"

"No," she answered reluctantly. She looked puzzled and then she continued, "Let's eat while we discuss it. The soup is ready. Maybe we'll come up with answers as we down the meal!"

As they ate, Rabbi Lamdan steered the conversation to the topic of Mr. Brenner. Moshe Katz shifted uneasily in his chair. "Mr. Brenner's son is not a well person," he said. "Whatever caused his paralysis will probably confine him for life. It's a tragedy, yet I sense that Chananya feels his father's love. When I see the two of them together, I sometimes step out into the hall to cry. Mr. Brenner has never cried in front of me or Chananya. He's a wonderful father." He frowned thoughtfully and placed his spoon on the table.

Rabbi Lamdan held up his own spoon as if to study it. He smiled at Leah's anxious face and bent toward Moshe Katz. "It must have been difficult for you to leave your home," he said quickly.

"No, I wanted to leave! I chose to leave!" he repeated almost angrily. "I saw my mother die that day, and I knew that I had to get away from Europe." He shook his head vigorously and banged his fist on the table. Rabbi Lamdan nodded his head sadly and grew pale, but Moshe Katz continued talking. "You should never have to see what I saw." He spoke rapidly. "It was horrible! Bodies all over! The screams and cries for help are locked in my brain. Worst of all, no one knew what to do or how to help the injured and dying."

Leah studied his face and saw the lines of unhappiness streaking across his forehead. "Didn't Hatzolah come?" she asked.

Moshe Katz gave a haunted laugh. "Hatzolah! You have such emergency medical teams here in America. They are not so organized in Europe." He swallowed hard. He thought for a moment. "I promised myself that I would learn what to do and I would know how to help! That's why I trained to be a competent caregiver. But it's not enough!"

Dodah Devorah broke the tension in the room. Her voice was gentle and low. "Yes, you have accomplished your goal," she said quietly. "And now Chananya Brenner needs your help and you are there for him." A spasm of pain flashed across her face.

Moshe Katz stared back at Dodah Devorah. He squinted and shook his head sorrowfully. Leah bowed her head and rubbed her forehead with her thumb and index finger. She was about to say something but then reconsidered and remained quiet. It was her father who spoke next.

"One never knows the workings of Hashem. Here in the United States the Hatzolah organization came into being because of someone's personal tragedy. Out of the ashes, we must rise again. Hatzolah is looked upon as a pioneer Torah organization whose goal is to keep people alive, for it is only the living who can perform mitzvos. Maybe, one day, you will find the solace you seek after your tragedy; and when you find it, then you will be comforted.

"You have that need to find an answer to your question: Why did this happen to me and my family? No one knows the answer to that question and no one can really satisfy such an inquiry. All we can do is say Tehillim and pray that Hashem will help all His children everywhere."

CHAPTER 6

THE MISSING PAPERS

The ringing of the doorbell startled everyone. Dodah Devorah left the kitchen, but soon returned with a nervous, haggard young man. He had light-brown hair, a sorrowful face, and cheeks stubbly with the shadow of a beard. At first glance he seemed to be in his 20's.

"He wishes to speak to you," Dodah Devorah nodded to Rabbi Lamdan and Leah.

The young man's shoulders slumped as he swallowed and took a deep breath. "My name is Shemayah Levin," he introduced himself. "My Rebbi, Rabbi Shalom Yaakov, suggested that I speak to you about a family matter." He began to cough uncontrollably.

Rabbi Lamdan immediately stood up and extended a hand. Leah filled another glass with water and centered the box of tissues on the table.

"Shall we go to my study?" Leah's father asked when the coughing subsided. The young man looked torn. He seemed confused, forlorn, and vulnerable.

He spoke in a high-pitched tone. "Please, I'm sorry to interrupt you when you are with your family but I got up from shivah just two days ago," he continued. "I still can't believe what is happening!" His hands twitched on his jacket as he curled his left fingers into a fist and rubbed them against his right arm.

Leah's father looked concerned. "Do you want to go to my study?" he repeated.

"No! No! No!" Shemayah Levine yelled impatiently. "I don't mind sitting here if you don't mind. It really doesn't make any difference to me." A shadow crossed his features. Leah asked if he needed anything else but he shook his head and closed his eyes momentarily. Then he began to speak.

"My father, zichrono livrachah, passed away nine days ago," he said quietly. He paused and wet his lips with his tongue. "He was murdered!"

"Oh, no!" They all gasped in horror.

"He was a private accountant in Manhattan. His office was down the block from the Diamond Exchange. He made a good living and supported our family comfortably. The police think that the murderer believed that my father had a lot of money in the office. But my father was just auditing books that evening. The police are still searching for clues, but they have not yet apprehended anyone." Shemayah Levine shut his eyes again. When he opened them, Leah saw the pain he was suffering.

"Do the police have any suspects?" Leah heard herself blurt out. "Why have you come to us?"

Levine glanced around the room and blew on his fingers as if he were cold. "We were raised as non-practicing Jews.

When I met Reb Shalom Yaakov on campus, I suddenly wanted to know more about Judaism. My father resented that. He wanted me to graduate and become an accountant like he was. He wanted me to work on Shabbos and Yom Tov. But I changed, and I wanted to learn Torah. He was very upset with me. He used to say, 'Doesn't your Torah teach you about respecting your parents and listening to what they tell you?' I never answered him rudely, but I also kept my Shabbos.

"My brother Izzy followed a different track. He joined a gang of hoodlums and was kicked out of high school. Then he left home."

Leah suddenly realized that her first evaluation of Shemayah Levine had been inadequate. She studied his face again. Although his eyes looked tired and frustrated, he was not encompassed with sadness. There seemed to be serenity in his soul.

"When my father saw how Izzy changed and what had become of him, although we really didn't know too much about his activities at that time, his attitude toward me changed. Sometimes while I would be reviewing some gemara that I had studied that day with Reb Shalom Yaakov, he would come over to me and ask questions. He began to think about observing some of the mitzvos. I think that I was lucky because he began to recognize the beauty of Torah."

Leah smiled to herself and placed her chin in her hand. Since Shemayah Levine had paused, she didn't think that he would mind her question. "How did your mother feel about it?"

"Mom was like my dad. She thought we should do what made us happy. She believed that you couldn't be happy doing mitzvos. She also thought that Izzy couldn't be happy hanging around with a gang of bums."

Leah looked puzzled and pulled gently on her earlobe. She had many unanswered questions swirling through her mind, the same questions she had asked herself when Shemayah Levine had first come into their home. *Why had he come to them? Did he want her father to influence his parents to keep Shabbos? Since his father was not alive anymore, did he want them to communicate something to his mother?* It was as if Shemayah Levine heard her unasked questions because suddenly his mood changed. He began to speak more forcefully.

"About two years ago Izzy disappeared without a trace. I know that my father hired a detective to find him; but if a person really wants to hide, it's not easy to find him. My father immersed himself in his work even more. He took extra auditing jobs, working day and night. Mom became a volunteer in one of the local schools. I was able to convince her to do in-house English tutoring at one of the yeshivah elementary schools. She began to understand my feelings toward Judaism. She liked working with the children and I know that the yeshivah is very happy to have her involved in their program. But Dad was really saddened by all that had happened. He took it hard. He had grown up believing that his children would follow in his footsteps; but here we were, his two sons, each going in a different direction, neither interested in his accounting business. I wanted to learn Torah, and Izzy had turned off to something else.

"Then suddenly, out of the blue, Izzy called. I was the one who answered the phone. He wanted to speak to my father, who was at work. He wanted to know where he was auditing because he wanted to stop in and see him. I wasn't sure that that would be a good idea, but he sounded all right on the phone so I figured that there would be no harm." He sipped some water and cleared his throat. Leah took his glass and filled it again.

"Since I wasn't exactly sure where my father was working, Izzy told me that he would call me the next day and I should give him the information then. He also asked me not to mention his call, as he wanted to surprise Dad. I remember shrugging and thinking what a surprise Dad would have!"

His fingers began to play nervously with the edge of the tablecloth as he paused to organize his words. "He called back two days later and I told him that Dad was working in his own office that week, so he could probably find him there anytime during the day and maybe even part of the evening. I asked him how things were working out for him, but I really wasn't sure what he mumbled back to me. It sounded almost like 'Baruch Hashem,' but I am pretty sure it was not that."

Leah studied his face while he was speaking. The strain was obvious. The furrows in his forehead deepened and dark bags indicating exhaustion were evident under his eyes. He looked as though he was suffering and in deep pain.

"Did they meet?" inquired Dodah Devorah. She looked pale. Leah looked back at her aunt. *She was a survivor,* thought Leah. *Dodah Devorah could encourage anyone.*

Shemayah Levine continued. "I believe that my father loved us very much. He wasn't the kind who showed his feelings, but we knew that he was always there for us. I think he expressed himself best in the letters he used to write to us when we were away at camp, on Boy Scout trips, or in the dormitory." Shemayah's face darkened. He looked anxious and displeased with himself. Leah was surprised at the change in his demeanor. Obviously he was coming to the part of the story that most disturbed him. Some of his words were mumbled and unclear. She strained to hear him.

"I don't know whether or not Izzy ever saw my father that fateful day, but someone else did. That person murdered my father during an attempted robbery, and my mother and I went into mourning."

The listeners gasped audibly. Almost in unison, in a reflex action, they said aloud, "Baruch Dayan HaEmes."

"Izzy called me yesterday," he continued. "I told him what had happened. He hadn't known. He was shocked. I heard the tremor in his voice. He seemed totally unprepared for my words."

"'How did it happen?' he asked me. He admitted that he had met my father that afternoon. Everything seemed to be all right. They promised to meet again, but Izzy had to settle some things first. He promised my father he would return after he finished some business he had to take care of.

"He cried on the phone. It was terrible. I cried too. I let my tears fall for my father, my brother, my mother, myself. I felt my heart would break." He heaved a heavy sigh. "Oh! May we all be comforted among the mourners of Zion and Jerusalem!" The outburst shook everyone. No one was dry-eyed; the tissue box was almost empty. Leah had a gnawing feeling inside.

"Why have you come to us?" she finally asked. "What do you want from us?" As she was prepared to ask yet another question, she suddenly stopped, cleared her throat, and frowned. She raised her eyebrows and looked into Shemayah's eyes. "Do the police suspect that there are too many coincidences?"

Shemayah Levine nodded his head sadly. "The police checked for fingerprints. My father's, my mother's, and mine are easily accounted for. Among other fingerprints were those of my brother. My brother has a police record, and he was listed as a runaway when he was younger. The police believe that he visited my father, they argued over money and then accidentally, they say, Izzy struck my father and killed him."

"What do you believe?" Leah asked sharply. "And your mother, what does she believe?"

"I have not told my mother about their suspicions," he replied.

Rabbi Lamdan frowned. This was an unexpected turn of events. He rubbed his hands against each other in anguish. "Do you want me to speak to your brother?" He looked at Shemayah long and hard, and then his eyes softened. Shemayah was pale.

"The police believe that Izzy may have originally wanted a reconciliation with my dad and then left, because right afterward, my father sat down and wrote Izzy a letter. I told you that my father could express his feelings best in the written word. My father kept a 4 x 6 pad on his desk to jot down notes. This time, he actually composed a letter to my brother. According to the police, my father must have been writing the end of the letter when Izzy returned. And then what happened, happened."

Leah bit her lip. Her head began to throb. She pinched the bone above the nose to relieve the pressure. "Where's the letter?" she suddenly asked.

"The police gave me a copy to prove to me that there was no reconciliation. They think that it's possible that my brother made up the whole story." His eyes looked down as his hand went deep into his pocket and emerged with four written pages. No one reached out to take them. "The truth is, whoever was there with my father really messed his place up. Papers were scattered all over the floor. Drawers and file cabinets were emptied as if someone were looking for something. The police assume that Izzy was looking for money. As I said before, the police found these pages and copied them. Maybe you can read something into them that I don't see," he added grimly. Suddenly tears welled up and washed over his face. He turned aside, embarrassed by his display of emotion.

"You must help me," he pleaded, trying to keep his voice from cracking.

"It's all right," responded Mrs. Lamdan in a hoarse voice. "It will be all right," she quickly corrected herself. Rabbi Lamdan looked at Shemayah with a calm steady gaze and took the pages of the letter. He began to read aloud:

> Dear Izzy,
>
> Recently, your name and Stanley's name came up in a conversation with Joe Harris. You may remember Joe, although maybe you wouldn't recognize him today with his short, stringy hair. Joe said that he had heard that I was not happy with the two of you and he wanted to give me encouragement. He told me not to lose hope. He even used a Hebrew expression meaning, "What the mind won't accomplish, time will." You used to call Joe "Plus Joe," remember, both because he loved math and because he was always in a positive mood.
>
> Anyway, I thought about you after you left today, and I was surprised and pleased that Stanley, now known as Shemayah, knew that you planned to visit me here at the office.

Stanley has changed so much since he became religious, but he still looks like your mother's side of the family. When you came into my office today I was surprised to see a younger version of myself standing in front of me. There are a lot of differences between us, but we have a lot in common, too.

I know that parts of our conversation did not come easy to either of us, but I know that I'm not ready to retire yet, and I need my earnings for your mother and our future. You and Stan are young, and you have your whole lives ahead of you. Your mother and I are happy with what we have and we are not ready to change our way of life. I have gone with Stan to his synagogue and I've met the people there. I found that they're just like people all over. They worry too. But what does amaze me is their love of Torah. I never saw anything like that before. In the middle of a discussion on baseball scores, they would suddenly pull out a gemara and sit down and learn ... and be totally focused on the big Talmud. Well, if it makes them happy, I'm glad for them.

Changes aren't easy. I know what you want from me, but I cannot commit myself at this time. I'm like the leopard who can't change his spots. Perhaps *you* are still searching; but as far as I'm concerned, the search is over. I'm sorry I can't give you what you want and obviously need, but I hope you realize that it's not because I don't love you, it's just because that's the way I am.

Yitzy, call us any time.

"That's it?" inquired Leah. "He doesn't sound upset with Izzy — or Yitzy, as he calls him at the end — in this letter."

Shemayah's voice was hoarse. "But it also doesn't sound like my brother left satisfied, does it?" He shook his head sadly. "The police believe that Izzy went back to get money from my father, and my father refused to give it to him."

"There could be another explanation," Mrs. Lamdan assured him. "It will come to us, I'm sure."

Rabbi Lamdan passed the letter to Leah and she read it again quietly to herself. "How did the police find the letter?" she asked. He looked at her, sighed, and wiped his forehead with the cuff of his shirtsleeve.

"The police said that when they arrived, the place was a mess. The files were strewn all over. They looked around to find a phone number, then they called us. I answered the phone, not my mother. I immediately went to my father's office. When I got there, the police handed me these four pages. They wanted to know about Izzy. I told them that he's my brother. I didn't tell them anything else. Then they asked me to look around and see if anything was missing. The only thing I knew that my father had in his office was his tallis bag, which I had bought him. That had been taken. That was about it."

"Did you ever find out from Izzy what he and your father spoke about?"

He punched the fingers of one hand into the other like a baseball player hitting his glove as he glanced out the window and then turned back to Leah. "He said that he told my father that he wanted to move to Israel. He said that he wanted to leave the past behind him and start anew. He wanted my father to retire, and he wanted my parents to join him on aliyah. He was sure that if they would go, then I would move, too. Being away from home had taught him to love home. And being on his own in the world had taught him to appreciate the good of mankind."

Rabbi Lamdan looked glum. He couldn't think of any encouraging words to say. Meanwhile Dodah Devorah stood up and went to the refrigerator. "I made a special treat for Rosh Chodesh," she announced. "Maybe my Rosh Chodesh kugel will unmuddle our brains." As she took out some plates and utensils to serve the kugel, Leah remained hunched over the letter.

"There are certain things about this letter that surprise me," she said, without looking up. "For example, why doesn't your father mention the fact that Izzy wants them to join him in Israel? Isn't this some sort of sign that your brother is seeking his roots? Your father pointedly mentioned Shemayah studying Torah, so why doesn't he mention Izzy's plans?"

Dodah Devorah sighed and passed a plate. "Do you think that that's why the police don't believe Izzy's story?"

Shemayah accepted the kugel Mrs. Goodwin had passed to him. He shifted in his chair and looked uneasily toward Rabbi Lamdan. The look on Leah's face was one her mother had seen before. She knew that Leah was thinking deeply about something. She waited and smiled to herself, because she recognized "the look."

"When did *Izzy* become *Yitzy*?" Leah asked. "I notice that your father referred to your brother as *Yitzy* in his last sentence."

"*Izzy* is short for *Isaac*, and *Yitzy* is short for *Yitzchak* who in English is called *Isaac*. My brother decided to start using his Hebrew name like I do." Shemayah laughed. Then he blinked again and stared at Leah. "Since my father referred to him as *Yitzy*, I guess that that's proof that he knew that my brother had become religious." He was excited now.

"But it doesn't prove that they didn't argue," Rabbi Lamdan said soberly.

Shemayah Levine gripped the handle of his fork and frowned. "What can I do?" he asked. "I know in my heart that my brother is innocent!" For long minutes, no one spoke. Dodah Devorah shook her head as she ate some of her kugel.

"It's Rosh Chodesh today," she said calmly. The calmness in her voice surprised Leah. "Let's think good thoughts for the month, and maybe good things will happen."

Mrs. Lamdan smiled and turned toward her sister. "This kugel is delicious," she said. "I guess that this is the one thing that a computer can't do."

Dodah Devorah laughed. "You can program a computer to do anything," she answered.

"Can it mix the ingredients for a cake or kugel?" Sarah Lamdan laughed.

"It can mix all the proper ingredients, but it can't taste it to know how really good it is." Dodah Devorah stood up and straightened her skirt. She looked directly at Leah and smiled. "I have a funny computer story," she said. "Want to hear it?" Leah nodded her head and pressed her palms together.

"Please?" she mouthed softly.

"About five or six years ago I met a Rebbetzin Moskowitz on Ocean Parkway here in Brooklyn. The Rebbetzin actually used her personal computer to help her husband print the sefer he had written. She did a beautiful job on the printing, and I told her so. She told me that she had stored many religious documents in her computer's memory, in case her husband, a Rav in the community, would ever need an important document as soon as possible.

"One Rosh Chodesh an elderly Russian immigrant couple came to him to be married. They wanted to be married according to Jewish law, because in Russia they had not been able to do so. The chupah ceremony started later than expected and therefore the kesubah, the marriage contract, that was already written had the wrong Hebrew date on it. The Rebbetzin went to the Rav's office, where the computer was kept, and printed out a new kesubah with the correct date. Then, the Rav noticed another mistake. The kesubah that she had just printed was for a previous groom whose name was Yisrael. This groom's name was Binyamin. The Rebbetzin had told one of her older children to change the *Yisrael* to *Binyamin* and print out a new kesubah. When the new kesubah was handed to Rav Moskowitz, he began to laugh out loud. You see, his son had instructed the computer to change all Yisrael's to Binyamin's so that the kesubah now read, 'according to the laws of Moshe and Binyamin,' when it should have said, 'according to the laws of Moshe and Yisrael.'"

Rabbi Lamdan began to chuckle and nodded. "The computer could not distinguish one *Yisrael* from another," he explained to Moshe Katz and Shemayah Levine. "That's a good story," he said. "I remember reading that someone once asked Rav Chaim Kanievsky how many times the name 'Moshe' appeared in the Torah. Rav Chaim answered immediately: 614 times. The questioner shook his head and said that the name Moshe is mentioned 616 times.

"Rabbi Kanievsky then replied that a computer counts words by recognizing the letters and not the pronunciation. There are two additional words in the Torah that are spelled like the name *Moshe* but they have different pronunciations and meanings. One of those words means 'from the sheep' and the other means, 'to lend.'"

Moshe Katz turned to face Rabbi Lamdan squarely. He smiled slightly as he glanced around the room. "I heard that someone asked Rav Chaim Kreisworth, *zt"l*, how many times the name of Bruriah, the wife of Rebbi Meir, is mentioned in Shas. Rav Kreisworth answered immediately, 'seven times.' The person who asked the question shook his head and frowned. 'Her name is mentioned only four times,' he contradicted. Rav Kreisworth shook his head and responded. 'You probably used a computer to count,' he said. 'You should know that four times the name is spelled with an *aleph* at the end and three times it is spelled with a *hei* at the end.'"

"I must remember to repeat this story to some of the computer experts that I meet sometimes. Computers obviously can't do everything. They can only process what we put into them."

Shemayah Levine frowned disapprovingly. He leaned over and mumbled something to Rabbi Lamdan.

"I wish we could help you," Rabbi Lamdan said wearily. His eyes fixed on Levine's sad brown eyes and then Rabbi Lamdan broke eye contact and turned his gaze toward his daughter. "Leah, why are you fidgeting? Is something wrong?"

"Yes," Leah said flatly. "I think something is very wrong. I find it unbelievable that Shemayah's father did not mention the change in Yitzy. That reminds me of something I learned in school about Rosh Chodesh." She gave her mother a broad wink and than began to explain herself.

"On every holiday, during davening, we add a group of psalms, the Hallel. On some holidays, such as the last six days of Pesach and on Rosh Chodesh, we don't say the whole Hallel. We omit two paragraphs."

"It's not exactly two paragraphs," interjected Rabbi Lamdan. "Hallel is recited because every festival has its own korban, an offering that indicates a new spiritual manifestation. The Prophets did not ordain that Hallel be recited on Rosh Chodesh, yet nevertheless the custom developed to recite the abridged version on Rosh Chodesh."

"Do you mean 'half-Hallel'?" asked Moshe Katz.

Rabbi Lamdan cleared his throat. "We call it half-Hallel although in reality we omit only the first eleven verses of Tehillim 115 and 116. Their general themes are repeated in the second parts of these two psalms, which are said when we recite the half-Hallel, so nothing essential is lost by their omission."

Leah nodded. She stood up and removed a Siddur from the "Bentcher Box" affixed to the wall.

"What does this have to do with Shemayah Levine's problem?" Dodah Devorah asked.

"Well," began Leah, "because today is Rosh Chodesh we say only half-Hallel." She closed her eyes as she tried to express her thoughts. Then she opened them and smiled. She turned to Shemayah Levine. "Your father's letter seems to me to be half of a letter. It is not complete. I have many questions about it. Many things seem to be skipped or ignored. Why didn't your father acknowledge this change in your brother? It's as if your father had much more to say or write and we don't have the entire letter."

"What are you saying?" asked Levine.

"I'm saying that I think that the police did not do a complete job when collecting all your father's papers. There is more to this letter than what you have brought us. The other page or pages will probably answer the questions that are lingering in my mind. This is a half-letter, like a half-Hallel. I think that you must return to your father's office and find the missing pages."

Shemayah Levine suddenly stood up and rushed to put on his coat, which had been placed on a chair near the entrance.

"I hope you're right," he called back as he moved out the door.

"Me too," said Moshe Katz as he watched Shemayah Levine leave. His eyes were blurred with tears as he studied the Lamdan family. "It's as if his father's love is reaching out to him from the grave," he said solemnly. "Please let me know what happens."

Then he, too, stood up to go. Suddenly he glanced at the clock on the wall. "I'd like to make a phone call," he blurted out. "I have my phone card with me, and I'd like to make an international call, if that's okay." He had a hangdog expression on his face. Rabbi Lamdan looked at him and pointed toward a phone. Mrs. Lamdan's eyes became pensive and moist.

"Use the phone in the study," she said quietly. "It's more private."

CHAPTER 7

LOST AND FOUND

Dodah Devorah walked over to the computer, picked up the printout, and frowned. "Shimon Brenner's description doesn't match anything stored in the mainframe database," she told them, "although it isn't unusual for the computer to turn up a blank."

Shimon Brenner is not what one may refer to as a common criminal.

"A penny for your thoughts," Mrs. Lamdan poured herself a cup of coffee as she looked at her husband's face.

"I have so many thoughts right now," he answered dully, "I can't even figure out which one is worth even a penny."

Mrs. Lamdan burst into laughter and then stared out the window. "Moshe Katz is a fine young man but he has suffered a great deal."

"Losing a family member is always terrible," Rabbi Lamdan agreed with a sigh, "but it seems to me that

Moshe Katz may have run away from his family. After his mother was killed, he just wanted to get away from his past and forget what had happened. But he forgot that running from this event in his past separated him from his family and their love and that is an even greater tragedy."

"Do you think that he is calling home?" Mrs. Lamdan faced her husband.

"I hope so, "Rabbi Lamdan rubbed his eyes. The beeping sound of the computer interrupted them.

Dodah Devorah grinned as she read the new printout. "Listen to this! There have been a number of jewel robberies in South Africa," she said. "Tiny stones have been smuggled into the United States."

"So?" Rabbi Lamdan looked down at his wristwatch. "What does that have to do with the disappearance of Shimon Brenner?"

Dodah Devorah studied the printout for a few moments. She sighed, then nodded her head. "A few days before each theft, Mr. Brenner was in that country."

"That's not real evidence," Mrs. Lamdan protested. "Mr. Brenner travels a great deal. There is no law that says his traveling must be related to a crime."

Rabbi Lamdan's eyes narrowed. Moshe Katz stepped back into the kitchen. He stared at the people in the room for a moment or two. "I spoke to my father," he finally said with furrowed brow. "I'm going back to London next week. We'll meet there. There are still many things that must be settled."

"Who will care for Chananya when you're away?" asked Leah. Moshe Katz's face reddened.

"I'll only be there a week, G-d willing. Mr. Brenner will have to make special arrangements. There are, thank G-d, many organizations that can help out."

"Yes," Mrs. Lamdan agreed. "Our N'shei group here is in contact with a group in Boston that also does chesed work. Are you returning to Boston first?"

Moshe Katz nodded. Then the phone rang. Rabbi Lamdan quickly picked up the receiver. He listened quietly. He reached into his pocket and pulled out a handkerchief, wiping his face as beads of perspiration appeared above his mustache.

"I understand, Lieutenant," he said solemnly. "Thank you for calling us. Leah and I will be on our way." Then he turned away and whispered quietly into the receiver, "G-d willing."

He cleared his throat and shook his head as he spoke to those around him. "That was Lieutenant McCarthy. They've found Mr. Brenner. They've taken him to the hospital again. He's very weak," he explained.

"Was he alone?" asked Leah. "Was he being held against his will?"

"The lieutenant didn't want to talk on the phone. We will meet him at the hospital."

Leah rushed to get her coat. She was happy for action and was hopeful it would lead to some answers.

"May I join you?" asked Moshe Katz. "I must tell Mr. Brenner my plans for next week."

Rabbi Lamdan took a moment to collect his thoughts. "Yes, please join us," he said. Then he turned to his wife. "I prefer that you not remain here alone. Perhaps your sister will stay with you."

"Of course," answered Dodah Devorah. "Just give the lieutenant this printout." She passed the computer information to him."

"I'm reluctant to take it," Rabbi Lamdan said. "These papers may implicate Mr. Brenner in a crime."

"On the contrary, maybe the information here will help him," Dodah Devorah said. "Anyway, the police will get these facts very soon."

With coats on, Rabbi Lamdan, Leah, and Moshe Katz turned to leave. Their footsteps were loud as they stepped outside. Leah began shivering from the cold. Rabbi Lamdan drove to the hospital. There they met Lieutenant McCarthy outside the lobby doors.

"A contraband shipment of diamonds, loose diamonds, is sent monthly from Europe to the United States. Interpol has been concentrating on these illegal deliveries."

"What does that have to do with Shimon Brenner?" asked Rabbi Lamdan.

"Brenner works for someone named S. Bishop. Mr. Bishop is the ringleader of the suspected smuggling ring. Bishop uses his jewelry connections to bring the diamonds in."

Leah gasped. She felt as if the pieces of a puzzle were beginning to fall into place. She was excited but she spoke slowly and carefully to be sure she gave accurate information. She repeated what Dodah Devorah had told her about the Mr. Bishop she had met on the plane coming to New York. McCarthy wrote this information in his little notebook.

Moshe Katz was taken aback. "This sounds scary to me," he said. "I can't imagine that Mr. Brenner associates with such people. Mr. Brenner is really an ehrliche Yid."

Leah paused to find the right words. "Lieutenant," she said as she turned to him. "Is there any actual connection between the two of them?"

"Funny that you should ask me," nodded the Lieutenant. "The Manhattan address you gave us is owned by Mr. Bishop. Two of our men went to his office. We believe that his office is a drop-off point for stolen goods."

"A drop-off?" Rabbi Lamdan's soft-spoken voice sounded tired.

"Thieves bring their loot there to get quick and easy cash. The thieves are usually kids who rob and run. This time, the officers found something there that is more serious. The kids murdered a man, a Mr. Levine, and dumped jewels and money into a tallis bag. It was easier for them to carry the stolen goods in it. Well, the tallis bag has a name on it. It's in Hebrew, of course, but one of our men who went to Bishop's place is able to read Hebrew."

"Shlomo Levine!" Rabbi Lamdan, Moshe Katz, and Leah said in unison. Lieutenant McCarthy's walkie-talkie suddenly interrupted them.

"Excuse me," he apologized as he moved to the corner to hear the caller. He spoke rapidly into his receiver. "Ten-four," he finally concluded as he returned to Rabbi Lamdan, Moshe Katz, and Leah.

"Yes," he said with a heavy sigh. "The tallis bag was identified. I originally thought that Levine's son was the culprit. But I guess I was wrong. The murderers are a gang of punks," he continued. "They get carried away with their violence and they don't think about the people they harm. Kids like these don't make it easy for us." He seemed resigned to it all. He stood quietly for a few seconds and then shifted his position.

"When the officers entered Bishop's place they found the tallis bag with the jewels and the tallis. A note was attached to the tallis; it's in Bishop's handwriting. 'Give to S.B.'"

Rabbi Lamdan cleared his throat and frowned. "Isn't that called circumstantial evidence? After all, S.B. doesn't have to stand for Shimon Brenner."

"Rabbi," laughed Lieutenant McCarthy, "you sound like a lawyer. Well, I'm going upstairs to ask Mr. Shimon

Brenner a list of questions, because now he is connected, albeit circumstantially, to a murder investigation, as well."

Leah's mind raced. She stared at Lieutenant McCarthy as she reviewed some of the statements he had made. "A shipment of diamonds is sent monthly from Europe," she repeated aloud.

"Yes," acknowledged McCarthy. "In fact, your Mr. Brenner knows plenty of people who are interested in buying jewels from abroad."

"Monthly? You mean, every month?" Leah looked wide-eyed. And then she snapped her fingers. "Today is Rosh Chodesh!" She dashed over to a calendar hanging prominently on the hospital wall. "This is a 2001 calendar," she said, disappointed. "I would like to see one for 2002. In fact, I would like to see a Hebrew calendar for 2002."

Rabbi Lamdan drew a laminated card from his inner pocket and passed it to his daughter. "I remember some of the numbers," she said, pressing her finger to her forehead. Then she carefully studied the Hebrew calendar with its corresponding dates and read aloud, "Rosh Chodesh Tishrei was Rosh Hashanah on September 9, 2002, Rosh Chodesh Cheshvan was October 7, 2002. Rosh Chodesh Kislev was November 6, 2002. Rosh Chodesh Teves was December 5, 2002 and this year, today is Rosh Chodesh Shevat, January 4, 2003. Today is a delivery day!"

When they approached Mr. Brenner in his room, he was a little drowsy from the medications he had been given. The lieutenant proceeded to read him his rights as he stared at the patient lying in the bed.

"I have nothing to say!" said Mr. Brenner. There was a tone in his voice that surprised Leah. It was cold and bleak and sent a shiver down her spine.

They all left the room, but then Moshe Katz asked permission to speak to Mr. Brenner privately. McCarthy squinted, frowned, and looked at Leah. "You go in with him," he said. "Maybe he'll soften up to the two of you. Since I represent the law, I may have scared him."

A policeman had already been assigned to stand guard in front of the door as Leah returned to Shimon Brenner's room with Moshe Katz. The old man was fumbling inside the night-table drawer.

"I need my Tehillim," he said desperately.

"Mr. Brenner," began Moshe Katz soothingly. "I must speak to you about Chananya."

Brenner looked furtively at the door. He lowered his voice to a whisper. "What's wrong?" he asked.

"I must go away for about a week," explained Moshe Katz. "You will have to make different arrangements for him for next week."

Mr. Brenner's eyes took on a frightened look. He shook his head and his eyes fell. "How can you do this to me now? It is so difficult for me. I don't know where to turn."

Leah moved forward. "Mr. Brenner, do you want me to contact someone for you?"

His eyes were pleading in his ashen face. "I'm afraid," he said. "I can't say anything."

He really is in trouble, Leah thought. *How could he possibly be connected to Mr. Bishop?*

"Please, Leah, call my nephew." Mr. Brenner's pleading voice was so low that, even standing beside him, Leah could hardly make out his words. "Call him," he coughed briefly. "He can help me."

Moshe Katz and Leah turned quickly and went out the door. Rabbi Lamdan and Lieutenant McCarthy had already gone downstairs. The policeman remained on guard in front of Mr. Brenner's room.

Moshe Katz and Leah walked to the elevator. "I don't feel right about this," he said.

"I don't either," Leah agreed. "Perhaps my father will drive by his nephew's house and see if he is home."

"But I can't wait," said Moshe Katz. He glanced around the hall. His voice took on a strident note as a dark wave of dread swept over Leah. "I must get back to Boston. Be sure to let me know what is happening. If necessary, I will change my plans and meet my father another time," he said quietly.

Rabbi Lamdan was waiting for them at the elevator as Lieutenant McCarthy stepped out of the hospital office with an old violin case. Leah looked at the worn leather case with the frayed handle that exposed the metal of the clasp. There was no doubt in her mind that it belonged to Mr. Brenner! It had scratches on it and a dent in the side.

"Has anything else happened?" she asked the Lieutenant.

"One of the owners of the coins is here in New York. We are trying to contact him. Maybe he can identify Mr. Brenner as someone he had seen before the theft. We are trying to build our case."

Leah drew in her breath sharply. She put her fingers to her lips and coughed lightly.

"Let's go!" Rabbi Lamdan said to her. "I must get back to yeshivah. I did not expect to take such a long lunch break." He shook hands with Moshe Katz and the lieutenant as Leah followed him to the car. "I'll drop you off at a bus stop," he said "as I must go straight to yeshivah. It may not be too difficult to walk outside now. I don't think that it is too slippery."

After he dropped her off at 53rd Street in Brooklyn, Leah telephoned her mother. She felt an odd sensation. This was where it had all begun — on 53rd Street in Brooklyn, when they had left Mr. Brenner near his nephew's house.

Dodah Devorah answered the phone on the first ring. "Leah!" Dodah Devorah almost shouted. Leah hadn't heard her so sounding so excited and happy in years!

"Leah, you were right! The fax just came in!" Dodah Devorah was breathless.

"What are you talking about?" Leah couldn't help but feel the excitement.

"Shemayah Levine!" was the excited reply. "He found another page of his father's letter and faxed it to us."

"Faxed it?" Leah questioned. "We don't have a fax machine!"

"You do now!" Dodah Devorah said brightly. "Your house is almost in the 21st century. I not only purchased a computer for you, but a fax machine as well. How else can people communicate with each other? If not by mail, then by telephone or fax!"

"So Shemayah Levine faxed you the page?"

"His father had a fax machine in his office. Shall I read the page to you? It's not long."

"Wait," said Leah. "I'm calling from a public phone. I'll run out of change!" She halted momentarily and watched a truck pull up to the curb.

"Oh, Leah, I'll have to get you a cell phone. How can you solve mysteries and not have one? I understand that you are only in high school, and a high-school student doesn't need one; but you, Leah, as a practicing detective, need one as soon as possible. Now, give me the phone number, and I'll call you back!"

After giving her aunt the number of the public phone, Leah hung up the receiver and waited. A large delivery van parked across the street. The phone rang and she picked it up immediately.

"Leah," began Dodah Devorah, "listen to this."

But Leah was watching someone moving in the car parked behind the van. She shook her head, trying to focus more clearly, and then decided that perhaps it was just her imagination. Her aunt had begun to read the missing page and Leah closed her eyes to concentrate better.

Dodah Devorah began to read. "'Now you tell me that you, too, have begun to understand Stanley's ideas. You want me to leave my job and join you in the yeshivah? I am sure that your Rabbi is a very interesting and articulate person, my son, but I am already used to my way of life. Stanley has taught your mother and me to keep Shabbos but the change is very difficult for us. How will we keep up with our friends if we become religious? My parents were religious people when they came to these shores. But I am not and I never have been. A leopard doesn't change its spots. It's hard for me to change my spots even though I am proud of you and Shemayah. Maybe, some day, after I retire, I'll sit down and learn some Torah. You know that every day now I put on tefillin. Shemayah bought me a tallis bag with my initials on it to keep my tallis and tefillin together. I don't necessarily put the tefillin on in the morning, but at some point during the day, I do. In fact, I'll go do that now and then I'll finish my work and go home. Thank you for your thoughts, my son. Welcome home.'"

There was a pause. "Leah, do you hear me?" asked Dodah Devorah. "Have you listened to what I read to you? I don't hear an answer from you."

Leah wiped a tear from her eyes and murmured sadly, "Baruch Dayan HaEmes for Mr. Levine's demise and Baruch Tov u'Meitiv for his sons. I guess this proves that Shemayah's brother and father were not angry with each other."

"Yes," replied her aunt. "The police now believe that Mr. Levine wrote this letter, then put on his tefillin, and then went back to his ledgers. The thieves placed all their booty into his tallis bag and tried to sell the whole lot to a Mr. Bishop. But they don't have conclusive proof that this Mr. Bishop has been the mastermind of everything."

Leah and her aunt heard a "beep" on the phone. "Oh, it's the call-waiting signal. Someone is calling," said Dodah Devorah. "I must answer the phone."

"That's okay," said Leah. "I'll probably be home soon. I'm in front of Mr. Brenner's nephew's house. I want to tell him the news about his uncle. Maybe he knows something and can help out."

"Sure thing," said her aunt. "Your mother is resting. She seems quite tired."

Leah watched the deliveryman go to the door of Ari Brenner's house. Was Ari Brenner home yet? The driver rang the bell while another man stepped out of the truck and began drinking soda from a can.

A young man answered the bell and stepped forward onto the sidewalk. "Bring it in!" he yelled at the driver.

CHAPTER 8

A SINISTER MEETING

The driver removed his cap and wiped his forehead with the back of his hand. Leah gasped. It was the man with the reddish-blond hair. Was he a doctor, a jeweler, deliveryman? Who was he? What was he doing here?

"Do you have the green?" the red-haired one shouted curtly.

"Of course," was the reply, "I got the green, and I mean green! Come right in." He managed a grin. The red-haired one turned to his partner and tipped his head sideways as a signal.

Leah's eyes widened as she watched this scene happening in front of her eyes. She bent down behind a parked car and took stock of the situation.

"Well, I have no time to waste. Are you bringing the stuff in or not?" shouted the man who had opened the door. "I can't wait here all day. It's cold out here!"

The men removed some boxes from the van and proceeded to carry them into the house. Leah's mind was in a whirl. She wished she had her own cell phone so that she could contact her father or McCarthy or even Dodah Devorah. Someone had to be told about this strange meeting. She could try to go back to the public phone and call Dodah Devorah, but she was afraid the men would see her. Fifty-Third Street was very quiet even though it was still quite early in the day. Most of the school buses had not yet begun their afternoons runs.

Leah glanced around the house and thought she saw a partially opened window near the side door. She ran forward. There was an empty crate nearby. She carried it to a spot under the window and stood on it. She peered cautiously through the window, her heart racing with fear. Would she be discovered? Her knees began to tremble. The owner of the house ... was it possible that the man at the door was Ari Brenner? She remembered seeing a picture of him in Mr. Brenner's wallet, but she wasn't sure that he was the same person. She could see him standing with his back to the window. He seemed to be arguing with the deliverymen, who were vigorously shaking their heads and holding their hands out for payment before putting down their packages. They seemed threatening!

Leah felt uncomfortable peeking through the window and, with feelings of guilt and shame, she stepped off the crate onto solid ground. She turned around to walk away while thinking what to do next, when she saw someone running toward her.

"Psst, young lady," he hissed at her. "Get out of here! We have enough trouble without you!"

The relief that swept over Leah surprised her. She had not expected this stranger's reaction to her. She closed her eyes and remained silent for a moment. The front door of the house suddenly opened. Leah's eyebrows lifted as she frowned and nodded thoughtfully.

"Quick!" the man said and hurried her across the street. His nose was running and his eyes were tearing with cold as his fingers clutched the cell phone he was holding. Seemingly from nowhere, cars converged on the street and men began running toward the van.

"See what I mean?" he said acidly. "You almost ruined everything and you would have gotten hurt, too." She looked at him for a long moment, lines of worry forming on her brow.

"Who are you?" she asked.

"I'm with the police," he answered quietly. "We've been observing you for a while. Why did you approach the house?"

Leah's face turned ashen. "Mr. Brenner's nephew ...."

"What's your connection to him?" the man cut in sharply.

Leah was speechless as she watched the police handcuff the man with the reddish-blond hair and his partner. An officer was talking to Ari Brenner. Yes! He was the owner of the house. Ari Brenner nodded and made his way toward Leah and the man beside her. Brenner nodded at Leah and said *hello* politely.

The two men shook hands and smiled.

"Mr. Klein?" Brenner said. "It's nice to finally meet you."

There was something about the name that made Leah gawk at the two men. "It was really touch-and-go," Mr. Klein said. "I was afraid for this young lady." He pointed at Leah. "There could have been some very serious problems."

Ari Brenner now turned toward Leah. "Who are you and why were you here?" His voice was deep and cool.

"Are you Mr. Shimon Brenner's nephew?" she asked simply. "He is not a well man, you know, and I wanted to find out how we could best help him."

Ari Brenner shrugged his shoulders. He spoke quietly. "My uncle, regrettably, has been out of a job for a while. He needs money to support Chananya. He probably could manage if he had to earn enough just for himself, but Chananya's bills are astronomical. I told him to place Chananya in a special home where he wouldn't have to pay so much, but he refuses to listen to me. When the Bishop group approached him to make jewelry molds, he jumped at the chance."

"Yes," said Mr. Klein. "But, when he realized that Mr. Bishop's plans were not 'kosher' he quietly contacted the police." His tone carried a mild reproof. "You know that your uncle is a very honest man, and he decided that although he needed the money, he would not compromise his ideals. So the police called Interpol and they contacted me."

"Why you?" asked Leah.

But Ari Brenner's head jerked up as he pointed an accusing finger at Leah. "Who are *you*? How did *you* get involved in this?" he asked. Just at that moment, a car drew up in front of them and screeched to a full stop. From the corner of her eye, Leah saw McCarthy, her father, and Dodah Devorah.

"Leah!" shouted Dodah Devorah as she emerged from the car. She ran to her niece and hugged her. "Lieutenant McCarthy got a message that a teenage girl was spying on Ari Brenner's house. They had to get her away from the house as the police planned a raid on those premises. The lieutenant wanted to know where you were because he felt that you were the only teenager he knew who might be interested in Ari Brenner's house. When I verified your presence, because you had just told me that you were here, he offered to pick us up and take us to you."

McCarthy and Rabbi Lamdan were talking to Ari Brenner. "Ladies," interrupted Lieutenant McCarthy, "I'm pleased to introduce you to Mr. Ari Brenner, our American connection to Interpol, and Mr. Aron Kleinkaufman, our European connection."

Suddenly all the crazy notions that had been spinning around inside Leah's head like the flashing colors of a kaleidoscope exploded into a great sunburst of light, and all the little bits and pieces settled into place and assembled themselves like pieces of a jigsaw puzzle. Now Leah was sure that she knew the secret of the stolen jewels. She didn't know how they had been stolen or by whom, but she was pretty sure that she knew what had happened.

Aloud she said, "The diamonds were sent to the United States every month. Mr. Brenner probably knows people who want jewels for special occasions." She stopped talking and then grinned from ear to ear. "Rosh Chodesh specials!" Her eyes twinkled as she pronounced the phrase again. "Rosh Chodesh Specials."

CHAPTER 9

A SECRET REVEALED

It was a pleasant afternoon eight days after Leah's experience with Ari Brenner. Dodah Devorah was packing her bags to return to London. Lieutenant McCarthy had stopped by to inform the family that Mr. Brenner was considered an unwilling accomplice and had therefore been released.

"Once Mr. Brenner realized that Bishop was a crook, he refused to work with him. Bishop threatened to harm Chananya. In a panic, Brenner told his nephew that he was worried about Chananya's safety. Ari contacted Interpol directly, since he had worked with them a long time ago. They contacted Mr. Kleinkaufman, who already knew about Bishop and had him under surveillance. Kleinkaufman wanted to know the identity of Bishop's contacts here. We told Ari to tell his uncle to work with Bishop one more time so he could be observed and followed by our men.

"We notified Kleinkaufman immediately. We informed him that he had to leave Paris right away. He removed a money envelope from his desk drawer and rushed to the airport to get a seat on Bishop's flight." Leah smiled at her aunt. "But he took the wrong envelope. He took the cash envelope that included credit cards in the name of Klein, while here in the U.S. he was known as Kaufman. He did not have enough cash with him and was in a quandary, when you saw his distress and helped him out. He panicked because the plane was ready to take off!"

"If Mr. Kleinkaufman is so famous, why didn't Mr. Bishop recognize him?" asked Dodah Devorah.

McCarthy smiled and sipped slowly from a glass of water. "On the plane Bishop did feel that Kleinkaufman looked vaguely familiar to him so he decided that he wanted to finish this job as quickly as possible. That's why he found it necessary to take Mr. Brenner from the hospital and find out if he had spilled the beans." He took another gulp. "Meanwhile, Mr. Brenner had been visiting his son in Boston. He left a message with Ari that he would be coming in and that he would work for Bishop one last time on condition that Chananya would be protected from it all. But Ari never got the message, as he was busy with his own contacts. That's why he didn't expect his uncle back in New York. When Mr. Brenner was hospitalized, Ari still didn't know anything. Bishop, in the meanwhile, panicked. He ordered the man with the reddish-blond hair to kidnap Brenner, threaten him, and order him to finish a new batch of jewelry molds."

"I don't understand," said Dodah Devorah. "What was Mr. Brenner doing with the jewels?"

Leah took a deep breath and grinned happily. "Mr. Brenner's job was to replace old links on the atarahs with new stolen jewels and then carry them to different drop-off points to sell."

Dodah Devorah's mouth fell open and Leah's eyes sparkled as she continued speaking. "Mr. Bishop used beautiful atarahs to carry his stolen jewels. Mr. Brenner would attach the jewels behind a link of an exquisite atarah. He would also attach a silver coin behind the jewel to hide it for traveling purposes. The atarah was not light but it could be carried comfortably in a bag. That's how the jewels and coins were smuggled into this country and sold here by unscrupulous jewelers."

"That's why Mr. Bishop was interested in my atarah?" Dodah Devorah was saddened by the thought that someone wanted to use a religious object in such an irreligious manner.

"As a man of taste, he sensed that your atarah would be exquisite," explained Mr. Kleinkaufman.

Lieutenant McCarthy sat down on a chair in the living room. He closed his eyes to stave off an headache. With his eyes still closed, he continued speaking softly. "Investigative work sometimes tires me out."

Rabbi Lamdan turned to Mr. Kleinkaufman. "How do you feel now?" he asked.

"It was my wife's yahrzeit a week-and-a-half ago," explained Mr. Kleinkaufman sadly. "This has not been a good year for me."

Rabbi Lamdan nodded his head and sighed. It had been a long day. He nodded to his wife. "Moshe Katz says that he will be on the plane returning to London," he explained, "and his father will be at the airport to meet his son."

"Oh, that's wonderful," Mrs. Lamdan said softly and then lapsed into silence.

Leah was happy that her mother was doing well. The doctor had told her the previous day that her leg was healing properly and rapidly. She found it a little easier to maneuver around than she had originally expected to. But perhaps it was the computer that had given her a new outlook on life. She could accomplish her necessary paperwork just by pressing a button. But, Leah knew, behind that button would have to be the human input to keep the computer alive and workable.

Suddenly Leah's mother had an interesting thought. She smiled and asked her husband. "Do you think that both Mr. Katz and Mr. Kleinkaufman will be at the airport at the same time?" she asked her husband.

"Your sister Devorah is going back on the same plane," he said. Then he shrugged and smiled. He was sure he knew what his wife was thinking. It was Leah who clinched it all by saying, "Everything is in the hands of Hashem. We just have to learn how to do His Will."

This volume is part of
THE ARTSCROLL® SERIES
an ongoing project of
translations, commentaries and expositions on
Scripture, Mishnah, Talmud, Midrash, Halachah,
liturgy, history, the classic Rabbinic writings,
biographies and thought.

For a brochure of current publications
visit your local Hebrew bookseller
or contact the publisher:

Mesorah Publications, ltd

4401 Second Avenue
Brooklyn, New York 11232
(718) 921-9000
www.artscroll.com